D
A *THE TRUMPET IS BLOWN*
V
I
D

L
A
M
B

I WRITE WHAT I LIKE, INC.
P.O. BOX 30
NEW YORK, NY 10268-0030

This is a work of fiction. Names, characters, places and incidents are either the product of the author's imagination or are used fictitiously. Any resemblance to actual events or persons, living or dead, is entirely coincidental.

Grateful acknowledgment is made for permission to reprint from:

"To see," by Saundra Lamb. Copyright © 1991 Saundra Lamb. Reprinted by permission of Saundra Lamb.

ISBN 0-9640692-2-9

Library of Congress Catalog Card Number: 97-093607

Printed in the United States of America

Dedicated to Richard Lamb (aka Big Ricky, alias Uncle Ricky)

Special Thanks to: My editor, Cynthia Ray Reddrick (even though I hate you (smile) for making me work so hard); to my assistant editor Marcus Allison once again, I could not have done it without you; to my line editor Janee Troutman (I'll never figure out how you caught all of those typos--great job); to Tracy Grant for not letting me forget (for one moment (smile)) that a story has to have a certain flow; to Terrence Jones for catching those little inconsistencies and to Nicki Marsh for the thumbs up.

There is a parallel with jazz and religion. In jazz, a messenger comes to the music and spreads his influence to a certain point, and then another comes and takes you further. In religion--in the spiritual sense--God picks certain individuals . . . to lead mankind up to a certain point of spiritual development. Other leaders come, and they have the same Holy Spirit [and pass] it to the next and the next and so on until there is peace and unity of mankind on earth as it is in Heaven.

Dizzy Gillespie

I don't like throwing God up into anybody's face and I don't like it thrown in mine. But if I have a religious preference, I think it would be Islam, and that I would be a Muslim.

Miles Davis

Some believe in Jesus, some believe in Allah
but players like me believe in making dollars

D.J. Quik

Now what's left when there ain't no God, just a whole lotta pride, might be a homicide, so let the drama slide, we don't want no problems B, catch your name in the obituary column sheet

Special Ed

Some Blacks smoke crack, poverty's search for ghetto heaven
Some Blacks sell crack to receive that which ain't given
The oppressor makes crack, then him push it in my home
'Pure Poverty' what I cry, Oh why? I wish pure poverty gone
Oh why, pure poverty gotta be what I cry?
Oh why, pure poverty gotta be what I cry?
Oh why, pure poverty gotta be what I cry?
Oh why? Oh why? Oh why?

Wise Intelligent
Poor Righteous Teachers

You always say,
"Don't tell me,
I have eyes,
I can see,"
and I think
to myself
tis' true you have eyes,
but I never saw you see

PROLOGUE

You ever go to church with your grandmother/ and
leave there with still more wonder/ You ever see
your great-aunt speak in tongues/ and as a little boy
wanna run/ You ever have your mom read the Bible
to you, and all the pictures are white/ like that's all
right/ You ever see a sista standing on the corner
singing about heavenly gardens/ while you're
catching the bus to kindergarten/ and come back
home to see her husband hitting the bottle's
bottom/You ever have a brotha pull your coat/ hip
you to the real dope/ pig that is/ and then have to tell
your mom, "I ain't eating no more swine"/ and
contend for her slow acceptance over time/ You
ever read about Mansa Musa, Mahmud Al-Kati/
Songhay and Mali/ You ever change your name and
have people think you're deranged/ insane/ to make
it plain/ "How you gonna function in a European
nation, wit' a non-European appellation?"/ You ever
read the Qur'an and get hit with the bombs/
destroying all the misconceptions/ a mental spiritual
resurrection/ You ever hang out with brothas
drinking forties and puffing, black/ but your head
was clear, 'cause you weren't down with that/ You
ever pray after a long hard day/ hoping that things
would change one day/ and then have it revealed
that the only way it will/ is if you make a change/
ain't that strange/ all this time you're looking
without/ and come to find out/ God gave you the
clout/ and you stand on the precipice of what lies
before/ and ask yourself once more what's in store/
and a little voice inside/ tells you to stand up and
rise/ above all the lies/ it's your time/ it's your time/
it's your time!

Chapter One

Back in the days, before the crack craze, before Jibril was Jibril (he was Chris then), before everything was real, before he'd sworn that swear that he'd forever wear as his cross to bear, Chris, like other little boys, wondered like Stevie (pun intended) what for Christmas would be his toy. He was just dying to know what the chubby-cheeked, ruddy-faced man in red was bringing him. Back then they were homeboys, he and Shaun. Back then everything seemed so simple and innocent, especially to two bright-eyed four-year-olds on Christmas Eve.

"Wussup, man, I know ya'll still awake, so stop frontin'. Hey, why ain't ya'll sleep yet?" Chris' older brother, Marcus, asked.

"I can't sleep, I gotta see what I got for Christmas," Chris and Shaun simultaneously implored in their excited, high-pitched four-year-old voices.

"Now c'mon, ya'll, ya'll know ya'll can't do that until tomorrow," Marcus said for the umpteenth time that night.

"Just a peek, I promise, just a peek," Chris begged, yet again.

"Sorry, man, wish I could help you, but moms would have a fit if she knew I let you take a peek and spoiled the surprise."

"I won't tell her, I promise! I promise!"

Marcus smiled, as he remembered making the same false promise when he was four years old. "Nah,

man, no can do, but I'll tell you what I will do, I'll make sure I wake ya'll up extra
early, okay? Is that cool wit' ya'll?"

"Yeah, I guess so," Chris said, while sucking his teeth in frustration.

"Good. Now, go to sleep, goodnight." And with that, the room door closed. The silence broken only by Shaun's emphatic declaration.

"Chris, your brother is so cool."

To Chris, Marcus was so cool! Chris worshiped the asphalt ground his older brother sauntered on. He wanted to be just like him. He tried to walk like him, talk like him--so did Shaun, after all, Marcus was like an older brother to Shaun as well. Chris and Shaun were so inseparable that Shaun's mother actually brought Shaun's gifts over to Chris' house late Christmas Eve, so that Shaun could spend the night and find his toys there in the morning. Without a father in either household, Marcus' stature grew even more in the boys' eyes, he was a legend in his own time. Before Run took a test to become an M.C., Marcus was sporting Kangols by the threes: one for the morning, one for the afternoon, and one for the evening. Before brothas in a project called Riverdale walked around with the fake Cazals, Marcus had two pairs. Of the real joints! Before Nikes had Air, Marcus rocked Clarks, Lord knows how many pair. And before Chubb Rock was so good he was bad, Marcus was so bad, he was terrible. Incredible.

The Trumpet Is Blown

Shooting hoops in the heart of Bed-Stuy, he'd drop rainbow jump shots from the sky.

Rainbow jump shots are a beautiful sight to behold; Jibril was still working on his. Sometimes he'd get the arc just right, and call the shot in midflight, right at its apex just before it would descend and he'd get to say yet again, "face job."

Sometimes a facial would be so sweet that there was no need to speak, you'd just walk away with a little extra hip in your hop, rub your index and forefinger under your nose while sniffing loudly with a sly smile, you wouldn't even have to say anything at all, everybody knew that the two finger sniff meant perfection. Perfection was what Jibril was constantly striving for on the trumpet.

Repetition, practice, breathing, playing. Repetition, practice, breathing, playing, composing. Repetition, practice, breathing, playing, composing, performing. Perfection. Practice makes perfect. Sometimes, late in the middle of the night, J.J. Johnson, trombone in hand, would pop up at the door of a young Miles Davis (then a student at Julliard) and ask the half-asleep, angry from having been awoken in the middle of the night Miles to hum Charlie 'Bird' Parker's latest tune until J.J., pen and pad in hand, could copy down all the notes, and then be gone like a ghost in the night. Repetition, practice, breathing, playing, composing, performing--like Miles, cool like dat!

3

"Yo', yo' Chris, what's up?" Marcus queried.

"Nuttin', Ah'm just lookin' at you exercise."

"Yeah, that's not all you lookin' at."

"What you talkin' 'bout?"

"Come here, give me ten pushups." Chris rushed over and got down into position, anxious to show his older brother that he'd been doing his prescribed two sets of ten pushups a day. "No, not like that, spread your arms out wider, wider. These are called wideouts, they're done to build up your wings." Marcus said, slapping the area under his muscular arms, just above his ribs and right below his chest. "Now, give me ten." As Chris began doing his pushups, Marcus playfully teased him about the night before. "So, I see you like lookin' at what Ah'm doin' in the livin' room. No, nope, don't try and talk, just do your pushups. I saw you crawlin' on your belly last night tryin' to peak in the livin' room to see what me and Pam were up to."

"No, I . . ."

"Don't try it, you busted."

"But . . ."

"But, nothin' you too young to be thinkin' about girls, boy."

"But, you're only fifteen."

"And you're only eight, so what you sayin'? There, since you did those ten so smoothly, give me another ten."

"Aw, man!"

4

The Trumpet Is Blown

The memories were coming back now, in waves. There was something refreshing about these early memories, they were happy and full of innocence. He came here today because it had been so long since he'd spoken to his brother, too long. He wanted to let him know what was up, that he was trying to take care of business and make their mom proud, like he'd promised to do the last time they saw each other.

"Wussup, Marcus," he started awkwardly, "it's been so long since we spoke, that I don't even know where to begin. Man, things is crazy out here, you know, so many things I dreamed of seemed to have soured wit' time, it's like the 'hood has become Beirut *knowwhatAh'msayin'*. Shaun, you remember Shaun? He's joined the other side. You made me promise to make moms proud, I'm trying. I'm about to graduate from high school, Music & Art. God willing, next year I'll be attending Columbia and Julliard. Don't tell nobody, but I've been working on an original composition for my Julliard entrance exam, shhhh, Ah'm a play a little for you, it's called The Trumpet is Blown, I got that from the Qur'an, but they won't know that. Well, here it go, I hope you like it." As Jibril played, the serenity he sought gave way to the passion of the music, and before long the painful memories he kept carefully dammed in the far corner of his mind, locked away as far as he could lock them, came flooding forth. He could see himself

5

playing ball. Oooh, that was a sweet move, smooth--with the left hand too! He was nice. Too bad those courts were all decrepit and whatnot, grass growing out of cracks in the cement, divots in the court, rim all bent. But there was no denying it, it was there on those messed up courts that some of the best games were fought. Brothas had to have 'ups', because that was the only way to get to the rim. The court was too sloped and had too many miniature hills, there was too much glass and too many dips and bends to get to the hoop by dribbling there. These were the courts the young boys were relegated to, those who weren't big enough or good enough yet to play on the new courts. These were the courts those who'd been slowed and weighed down by too many forty ounces over the years were relegated to, too. It was there that Chris and Shaun's developing games first began to emerge, the young boys playing against some of the old has beens. (Never was? Nah, that's too cruel.) Of course, not only was the court in need of repair, but the ball needed some help too. It wasn't meant for an outside court, and had developed lumps that looked malignant. If you didn't know how to play with a lumpy ball then you were in as much trouble as a politician trying to guess which way the voters were leaning. When you wanted to go left, the ball would go right, and when you wanted to go right, the ball would go left. And please don't let one of the lumps land off a missed shot in one of the divots! On top of

The Trumpet Is Blown

the lumps, the ball they were playing with on this particular day had too much air and you had to be careful not to bounce it too hard or it would go over your shoulder and you would get called for 'palming' or 'carrying' (two calls the refs in the NBA seem to have forgotten). Now, Jibril still hasn't been able to figure out (all these years later) what made Shaun think he could have made that jump shot, on that court, with that ball--on that day, with a slight drizzle coming down. Shaun, however, thought that he could. As his wayward shot careened off the top of the backboard, hopped over the fence and ran into the middle of the street the players watched, helpless, as a truck put an end to their beloved ball's agonizing life. "Kaboom!" They never thought that a basketball could make such an explosive sound. They were all in a state of mild shock--the way little boys can be when their favorite team loses--here one minute, the ball was gone the next. Before they had time to properly mourn the ball, everyone's attention was suddenly pulled toward the mass of people running by.

"Yo' Keith, what's everybody runnin' for?" Chris asked.

"Some kid is threatenin' to jump off the roof."

"Yo' Chris, c'mon!" Shaun said excitedly.

Why were they so drawn toward the macabre? If it's true that misery loves company, then in the ghetto, company loves misery. Nothing brings folks out like a rumor of a good fight, a bloody shooting, a bloodcurdling bus crash, a tumultuous eviction, domestic discord, a dogfight--in other words anything loud and violent. As he ran with the crowd that day, Chris was terror-struck. He didn't know why, but he was suddenly filled with a dread he'd never known. By the time they got there, whoever was threatening to jump off the roof had already made good on their tragic promise.

From six stories above, the beauty of nature suddenly became strikingly apparent to the leaper. As he leapt from the gravel-strewn roof, the whiteness of the sky's blue fascinated him. He'd never before noticed how truly beautifully the forest green of the trees and bushes contrasted with the earth's rich brown tone. Only a genius could have sketched such beauty, he thought, before abruptly painting the gray cement red.

Excited onlookers gathered round the broken body straining to view the ghastly sidewalk mural.

Shaun and Chris, too, maneuvered their way through the crowd hoping to glimpse this real life horror. Shaun arrived first, and by his horrified gasp, Chris knew.

Marcus had decided that he couldn't take it anymore.

Chris trembled with sadness, humiliation, and heartbreak, as he approached his brother's broken body, dying but not yet dead. He knelt over his brother unable to utter a sound, the pain was so unspeakable. In the midst of his delirium, his eyes now puddles of pain, Marcus recognized Chris. With waning strength he reached out and grabbed his younger brother by the wrist. Arms once large and powerful, now skinny and withered; skin once dark and unmarked, now ashy and scabbed. Between pain racked coughs, Marcus told him how sorry he was. He told him to say goodbye to their mother, and then he shook Chris, shook him with whatever strength he had left, and made him promise to stay away from crack, to stay away from drugs. And to make something of himself; make him proud and to look after their mother. Then he died, just like that.

The wake was held at Bethany Baptist Church. Jibril's mother looked worn. She blamed herself. It was her fault, she thought. Maybe if she hadn't thrown him out, maybe she could have gotten him to go into another rehabilitation program. Chris tried to console her, but all she had left of Marcus was grief and guilt; she couldn't let anyone take those away.

He sees himself walking toward the coffin, slowly, feeling all eyes on him. Some older women give him subtle, comforting smiles. He's getting closer, he's breathing heavier, this is it, he's going to kiss his brother goodbye.

Things changed with Marcus' death. Jibril's mother embarked on a mission to ensure that what happened to Marcus would never happen to Chris. He was in the seventh grade, and back then he would come home after school like everybody else, with no homework, or so little that he was out playing ball by 3:30, but he wasn't going to be spending every afternoon playing ball anymore. The next thing he knew, his mom had him taking trumpet lessons. Looking back now, Jibril was forced to smile to himself when he recalled those first lessons--how skillfully Hassan interweaved his trumpet instructions with lessons drawn from such seemingly disparate sources as Islam and basketball. When his mother first brought it up, Jibril didn't mind learning to play the trumpet; in fact, he thought that it would make him look kind of cool, but once he started, he couldn't get into the practice regimen Hassan was trying to impose on him. "Practice, practice, practice. Practice makes perfect." Hassan would say again and again in his booming baritone. "Would he give it up already?" Chris thought. No, he wouldn't. Hassan was like a gentle pitbull when it came to the development of his students, both musically and spiritually, for to him the two were intertwined. .

"You see Chris," Hassan would begin, "daily practice is an absolute requirement so that good technique becomes instinctual, you don't even have to think about it, you just have good technique because you've put in so much practice. Whether you're playing in front of people or playing in a studio, you don't want to have to worry about technique, you want to have made good technique habitual by constant practice. Once you've got technique mastered then you can start thinking about making great music. It's like this, see, I as a Muslim pray five times a day. Now, a lot of people say, 'dag, why ya'll gotta pray so much?'"

"He must have read my mind," Chris thought.

"What they don't understand," Hassan continued, looking at Chris as if he had read his mind, "is that prayer is moral and spiritual training. Like we exercise our bodies to become and to stay strong, we need to exercise our will, in order to become stronger spiritually. Constant prayer helps us to eventually be better people, just like constant practice helps us to eventually become better musicians."

Hassan could see Chris' face covered by a kind of glassy-eyed, not-fully-comprehending look, so he sought to explain himself on a level that a seventh grader could better understand.

"Okay Chris, let me break it down like this. See, it's like developing a great jumpshot or becoming a great free throw shooter. You want to shoot the ball over and over and over, until you don't even have to think about it--until it just becomes habit--second nature, natural."

"Oh, I see."

Chris could relate to that!

"So, are you going to start practicing, like I said?"

11

"Okay, yeah, I'll practice."

"That's my boy."

Every now and again, Jibril liked recalling the old days.

The Trumpet Is Blown

Chapter Two

Jibril practiced day and night--way into the night. Sometimes the neighbors would complain because he kept them up with his playing. His mother worried that he was becoming obsessed, and wasn't getting enough rest. To subdue the neighbors' complaints, and to lessen his mother's worries, he taught himself to practice by moving the keys while not blowing into the trumpet. To the outside world no sound was made, but he could hear the notes loud and clear. He replayed Hassan's lessons over and over in his mind as he sat there in the dark, "keep your hands near the keys, so you can play faster," he could hear him say. He'd started studying yoga breathing exercises a few years before, after reading that John Coltrane had done so to improve his breathing. Like Coltrane, Jibril would stay up deep into the night sitting statue-like, motionless, with his long, slender fingers tucked in his ears, intently listening to the various sounds emanating deep from within his body and mind, so that he could express them in music. This wasn't always easy living in the Terrordome, as his meditation would ofttimes be interrupted by erratic gunfire--gunfire which, ironically, planted the seeds of hip hop rhythm in his subconscious.

In the mornings, he'd listen to his favorite trumpet solos, studying them until he had them down--the timbre, the pitch, the tone, the emotive qualities.

He would tape himself playing these solos so that he could listen and critique himself later, and learn how to play it the way he wanted it to sound. Sometimes when his man, Bilal, would come by he'd find Jibril laying on the floor next to his bed, sometimes made, sometimes not--under the watchful gaze of Malcolm, of Duke Ellington and of Dizzy playing at Kenya's independence celebration--with like six books open simultaneously. He'd be reading about Islam, about African-American history, African culture, Algebra and Geometry--for some reason ever since he'd read Miles' autobiography he'd been on this math kick. Before then he had studiously avoided math, but after reading Miles he saw more clearly the connection between music and math. On his way to and from school he listened to whatever his favorite Hip Hop jam of the moment was, rewinding his walkman repeatedly, trying to figure out how to marry the best of Hip Hop and Jazz. He loved the way A Tribe Called Quest fused their music with jazz trumpet samples. And loved the fact that they named their second album <u>The Low End Theory</u> saluting their use of the bass, the same way Coltrane had named <u>Giant Steps</u> after its loping bass line. He had tried to get put down on Guru's <u>Jazzmatazz II</u> album, but things hadn't quite worked out. In spite of this, his many hours of practice finally seemed to be verging on paying dividends. His group's demo was making noise on the underground scene and it seemed just a matter of time before a label snapped them up. Meanwhile, Betty Carter's 'Jazz Ahead' concert, featuring the best young Jazz talent in the U.S., was fast approaching, and Hassan was confident that Jibril would be chosen. It was a long tunnel, but finally, if he looked long and hard enough, there seemed to be some light at the end of it.

David Lamb

Chapter Three

"Mr. Phibbs! Mr. Phibbs!" Like a seasoned weather vane being blown about in high winds, Jibril's upraised right hand waved wildly in the air trying desperately to attract his teacher's attention.

"Yes, Jibril, what is it now?" With an exhaustive sigh punctuating his exasperation, Mr. Phibbs reluctantly recognized Jibril.

"Why does the book say that Egypt is in the Middle East, when it's in northeast Africa?"

"Well, that's because North Africa and sub-Saharan Black Africa are two entirely different, separate, and distinct entities, with different histories, cultures, and peoples." Mr. Phibbs had to smile at the succinctness of his answer. "That'll teach him," he thought, until Jibril retorted without raising his hand.

"But, but Mr. Phibbs what do you mean, Black Africa? Weren't the first Egyptians black?"

"No, they were white." If this were poker, no one would have been able to tell what kind of hand Mr. Phibbs was holding.

"Excuse me? Well, what about Anwar Sadat?" Jibril said confidently, aware that his classmates' eyes were on him.

"Sadat was white!"

"Wait a minute," Jibril said with a light chuckle, "you know it's bad enough for you to say that the ancient Egyptians were white, but they're not

16

around, while Sadat just died a short while ago. I've seen pictures of him. Are you telling me that if Sadat were walking down 125th street today you'd say he's white?"

Sheepishly and defensively, but with deceit in his eyes, Phibbs responded: "He's white, according to science."

"Who's science?" Jibril asked, but before he could follow up the bell rang ending the class. Mr. Phibbs was as happy as an overmatched boxer, hearing the final bell signaling the end of the fight, knowing he had finished on his feet.

Mr. Phibbs was notorious for his penchant for twisting history to suit his vision, and he and Jibril had constant run-ins, especially after Jibril changed his name. What really irked Jibril was that--if you let him--Mr. Phibbs would always tell his tall tales with a straight face. No--make that a smile. And would react with alarm that anyone would actually question his veracity, let alone his accuracy. For Jibril, however, Mr. Phibbs' appearance spoke volumes. His slightly yellowed teeth reflected the yellow journalism that he passed for history. His smudge-marked glasses explained his distorted vision, and his ever whitening hair now covering his once black roots was symbolic of his attempts to whiten Egypt's Black roots. When he first changed his name, Jibril's mother was afraid that his grades might suffer from teacher hostility, and while he had maintained his grades, Jibril definitely

17

noticed an extra level of iciness since the change--suddenly he had an attitude problem, and this from teachers who before lavished praise on his attitude. No matter, he couldn't stop himself--he loved catching Phibbs in the midst of inaccuracies, just to see that annoyed, contorted, bewildered look on his face. It was like a sport to him, he'd even composed an ode to Mr. Phibbs' fanciful fables: 'Little White Lies':

Little White Lies cover fertile soil like snow,
freezing a young brotha's mind so it can't grow,
instead of reflecting the light of truth,
His-Story eclipses ours right at its roots,
so like a farmer pulling up weeds,
I weave through tangled webs that deceive,
'cauz the garden of my mind contains the freshest of
fruits,
and my thoughts and ideas are like well-armed troops
loaded with laser sight, ready to shoot the white lies
down from their pedestal
then watch as they crash land
sweep up the pieces, put 'em in the trash can,
standing tall, cause Ah'm like a rubber ball
the harder I'm dashed, the higher I rise
above and beyond those Little White Lies

"What up Carlos, I heard you had a run in wit' Mr. Phibbs?" Jibril asked in between bites on his traditional after-school butter cookie.

"Nah, it wasn't nothing really. I just had to set the record straight."

"Want a cookie?" Jibril asked, extending the open pack to Carlos.

"Yep."

"What happened?" Leaning in left ear first, Jibril was trying to soak up all the wonderful details.

"Well, he heard Mark call me by my middle name, and he asked me what's a Spanish kid doing wit' a name like Malik."

"No, he didn't," Jibril said mockingly, sarcastically drawing back in shocked indignation.

"Yes he did."

"He be buggin'. I had to get on his case earlier today about that mythical white Egypt shit."

"Yeah, I bet. So anyway, I told him first of all, Ah'm not Spanish, Ah'm Puerto Rican, and crazy Julio who sits in the back of the class gave me one of those old school Arsenio barks," Carlos said with a chuckle, his bop becoming more pronounced as he grew happier recalling his small moral victory.

"That's funny. Cookie?"

"Nah. Anyway, I told him how my pops had gotten interested in studying his family's roots, because of the influence the Young Lords had on him when he was younger. And that he learned that our last name, Medina, had roots in Arabia--that it was the city, Prophet Muhammad, peace be upon him, fled to

19

after the disbelievin' Arabs chased him out of Mecca. And then, to be honest, since he'd given me the opening I took the liberty to drop a little knowledge. I pointed out how when you see a Spanish-speakin' person in some sort of distress or difficulty and they want to ask God for help, you'll hear them say 'Ojala' which translates into English as 'Oh God', but really if you break it down, 'Ojala' is 'Oh Allah', which just goes back to that Moorish influence on Spanish civilization, which takes us back to Africa."

"Damn, you got all that in?!"

"Yep, he never even saw it comin'. It was beautiful, because not only did I get to set him straight, but I got to drop something on a lot of my Latino peeps, who be asking me how Ah'm gonna be a Puerto Rican Muslim."

"Ah'm proud of you, son."

"I just hope he don't mess wit' my grades now. Yo', remember when you first changed your name and he kept mispronouncing it?"

"Yeah."

"What was it he called you? Jibrel? Jabrel?"

"No, no."

"No? Oh yeah, that's right, Gerbil, that was messed up yo', but it was mad funny, Gerbil," Carlos couldn't help laughing. "And then," he said still laughing, "and then on top of that, somebody drew a picture of a gerbil wearing a kufi and playin' the trumpet on your locker."

"Yeah whatever, jus' watch he's gonna change Malik to Mikey." They both laughed.

"Yo', Gerbil, let me get that last cookie?"

"Forget you," Jibril said as he passed Carlos the golden, crispy, butternut-filled chip. "On the real though, be careful, he could be a problem. But check it out, I got to run see Hassan. I'll rap to you later. Peace."

"Peace."

As he rode the train back to Brooklyn, Jibril was glad that he'd decided to go to school in Manhattan, just to see something different--different places, different people. His classmates came from all parts of the City. So many of the people he knew in the projects never left. Virtual vertical Bantustans, they were worlds unto themselves. People who didn't live there never went, and people who did rarely left.

21

David Lamb

Chapter Four

"Yo' Jibril, yo' Jibril, oh it's like that now, you just gonna walk by a brotha without even stoppin'?" As soon as Jibril saw Kwame, he had to smile. His upraised arms stretched out widely to either side, his palms turned inward toward his head which was thrown back in exaggerated exasperation all told Jibril how happy Kwame was to see him.

"Nah, Kwame, it's not like that, you the man, I didn't see you. I was just in a rush." Jibril smiled while banging fists with the older brotha.

"What's going on, man?" Kwame asked as fist banged again. "I haven't seen you or Shaun by the gym in a long, long time." For as long as Jibril could remember, Kwame had been the director of the after-school program at his old junior high school. When they were in the eighth grade, every Tuesday and Thursday night without fail Chris and Shaun could be found, along with a host of other young brothas, working off steam playing basketball at the gym. And Kwame could be found, preaching and teaching lessons about life, liberty, and the pursuit of some jumps hot.

"Nothing much man, I've just been caught up in my music lately," Jibril answered, tapping his black trumpet case.

"Oh, okay, I just wanted to make sure everything was all right. How's the music comin'?"

The Trumpet Is Blown

"It's comin' together. It's comin' together."

"That's good."

"But, hey check this out, I've got a funny story for you. Remember that history teacher I was telling you about? Remember? Remember the one who I said was dissin' Marcus Garvey?"

"Oh yeah, Mr. Liar," Kwame said with a beaming smile, rubbing his goateed chin with his right hand anxious to suck up the glorious details of a good story. "What did he say now?" As Jibril relayed Mr. Phibbs' division of Africa, and his assertion that not only were the ancient Egyptian's white, but that Anwar Sadat was white, Kwame could only smile. It was like history repeating itself. More than ten years had passed since he'd graduated, and the same untruths were still being put forth. "See Jibril," Kwame said through a knowing smile, "what you've got to understand is that a young person's mind is like a blank blackboard, and people are just trying to write--with white chalk--what they want you to think, on that board. Now you've heard of the Zulu nation right?" Jibril answered in the affirmative, because Kwame had put him up on Shaka when he was in junior high.

"Well," Kwame continued, "Shaka had a great-nephew named Cetewayo who inherited the kingdom, and was a great leader and warrior in his own right. He wiped the British out at the battle of Isandlhwana, and in one battle killed Prince Napoleon, who was the heir to the French throne. Well, once a missionary tried to frighten him into converting to Christianity by telling him about hellfire. Cetewayo laughed and told him that his soldiers would stomp it out. He took the missionary out to a big ol' field, had the field set afire, and then told one of his commanding officers, "Before you look at me again, eat up that fire." And in a split second thousands of soldiers leaped onto the fire, barefoot, and stomped it out. That's what you gotta do to those little white lies, Jibril, stomp them out!"

"Yeah, ah-ight, chief, I'll jus' make sure I've got my Timberlands on," Jibril said with a chuckle.

"But hey, yo', I got to go. I'll catch you later."

"Later twelfth-grader."

Walking past the 'pharmacists', taking no shorts and offering no discounts, Jibril nodded as he passed by Shaun. At that moment he knew Melle Mel was right when he said 'it's like a jungle sometimes' and it made him wonder how he kept from going under.

The Trumpet Is Blown

Chapter Five

"Hassan, how's my favorite younger brother doing?" Ware asked as he slapped Hassan square on the back like a doctor urging a patient to cough.

"Don't you mean your only younger brother?" Hassan teased as he and Ware walked down the steps to Hassan's basement studio.

"Yeah, but you still my favorite," Ware said with a Coke and a smile. "I was checking out your paintings as I came down the steps, that last one is *bad*. You ever think about selling any of this stuff?"

"No, not really, I do it for relaxation. You see that piece over there? No, that one over there," he said with a sense of joy, his finger pointing the way past the photo of him blowing with Art Blakey, past the collage of articles reporting on the banning of 'Biko Lives' in South Africa.

"Wow, that's really bad, Hassan, and I'm not just saying that." By the gentle bobbing of his head Hassan knew that his brother had been touched--even if he hadn't said a word Hassan would have known.

"Thanks, coming from you that means a lot."

"That's Africa in the form of a horn, right?"

"Yep, I call it 'the Horn of Africa'," Hassan smiled at the play on words. "Sort of gives a whole new meaning to that term. Yeah, see, I got inspired to do this piece when I was in South Africa. Remember when I recorded 'Biko Lives', and it was banned in

David Lamb

South Africa? Well, you remember, years later I got invited down to play at Mandela's inauguration. It was good to play with some of them South African brothers and sisters I hadn't seen in so many years-- those brothers and sisters over there have a uniquely beautiful harmonic sense. Anyway, while I was down there I got turned on to the African art scene. The colors and shapes, the emotional depth conveyed, the pain and the hope in the same scene. When I got back to the States, I started working on this piece."

"Well, I really think that you *really* need to think about displaying these pieces."

"I'll think about it."

"You know, looking at that horn, I just thought of something funny." Shaking his head, Ware chuckled to himself. "These kids today, boy they think they invented everything. Listen to this," he said, almost whispering, his voice slowing down as if still amazed by the story he was about to tell, "a couple of weekends ago I was down in my basement listening to some Coltrane, and my dear son Malcolm comes down to borrow some money, of course. So he sits there for a bit listening, and then all of a sudden he jumps up all excited and he's like, 'Pops, I got some funky stuff for you to check out.' So he pops in his tape and I'm listening when it dawns on me who it is, and I ask him if he knows who he's listening to. He said, 'Yeah that's hip and hop.' Some rappers. So I tell him, 'No, my boy, that's your uncle, Hassan.' Some of these

26

young boys had taken a horn riff of yours from
Black&Blue. So I pulled out the album to let him
know that the old man was still cookin'."

"Well, all right!"

"Can you dig it!" Then they slapped five the
way the brothas used to do it back in days when Black
Power was on, all heartfelt and warm with multiple
forms. "You know what I'm saying, Hassan, these
kids nowadays, I just don't know what to make of
them. They jus' don't have no respect, for themselves
or for anybody else." Ware's face was covered by a
look of almost righteous indignation. "Back in the
sixties our singers used to have names like 'The
Supremes' and 'The Miracles', names that said
something positive and great, but look at these young
cats nowadays, it's like they've lost their minds. I was
listening to Malcolm listen to this cat the other day-
-'Dirty Old Bastard'. Well, anyway I thought it was
'Dirty Old Bastard', so I asked Malcolm why anyone
would want to be called that. And he looks at me, all
exasperated because I didn't get it, and he says 'it's,
not 'Dirty Old Bastard' it's 'Ol' Dirty Bastard'.' So I
say, whatever, why would anyone want to call
themselves that?! And now he's really frustrated and
he says, 'You just don't get it, he's old because his
style is ancient and he's a bastard because there's no
father to his style-- his way of rhymin', he originated
it himself; he didn't copy off of anybody. He's just
lettin' you know that he's an original whose style goes

way back.' So I'm thinking, my son is really spending far too much time thinking about this stuff--and I tell him that. And he says in a huff that I jus' don't see how deep it is. So then we got into it about those other cats, those, those gangsta rappers, what are they called 'Niggerish Attitudes'. . ."

"Actually, I think it's 'Niggas Wit' Attitudes' . . ."

". . . and those other guys, Naturally Naughty . . ."

"You mean Naughty by Nature'."

"And those girls, 'Sugar & Spice'."

"Sugar & Spice? Sugar & Spice? Oh, oh, you mean Salt & Pepa."

"Yeah, Pepa & Salt, why that girl got to have blonde cornbraids, jus' what is she tryin'a say?"

"I don't know."

"In my day, our women would never have paraded on a TV screen half-naked like that, shaking whatever, whenever, wherever for whoever. And that other guy, 'Ice Cream'? You know, that boy that was in that movie *Boyz in the Hood*?"

Hassan had to laugh at that one. "You mean Ice Cube?"

"That's the one. Boy Hassan, I don't know how you keep up."

"Well, you know, if I'm going to communicate with these young cats, I have to keep up. I'm trying to help guide them on a better path, in terms of what they say, the depth of their musical expression, and their understanding of the music business as a business. So, I've got to keep up. Hopefully, I'm able to provide some spiritual direction, some educational direction, and some pride in themselves and African people. I think that has value. And hopefully, the time's not far off when I can take steps toward really creating a full scale institution."

A full scale institution, 'The Freedom Jazz Institute', was Hassan's dream. He'd been talking to Imam Aziz about putting up $15,000 of his own money to purchase a partially boarded up brownstone that had become a haven for crackheads around the corner from the Al Qiyamah Mosque. Once it was renovated, the property would be worth far more than $15,000, but by holding onto the property the City was losing tax money and so was eager to put it in a taxpayer's hands. Although there were other properties in Bed-Stuy that Hassan thought might be more suitable, he ultimately settled on the building around the corner from the mosque in order to support its neighborhood development efforts.

He had gone through all of the paperwork-- now he just had to decide if he was really committed to removing the pookies who were using the building for a crack house. He'd spoken to Imam Aziz, and

David Lamb

he'd promised whatever help Hassan needed.

"So anyway, Hassan," Ware continued, "how's progress on the school coming? I know you've been at it a long time."

"It's coming along. You know, it's still in the planning stages, trying to figure out location, funding, financing, developing a curriculum, getting competent, inspired staff. I think that I may have found a way around some of those funding issues though . . ."

"Oh, really, what's that?"

"Well, remember I told you about that young brother I was thinking of asking the Imam to back for Congress? Well, one of the primary reasons I want to back him is that he's in favor of school vouchers."

"School vouchers?"

"Yeah, that's where the state provides a voucher based on the money it spends per pupil in the public schools, and then gives parents the option to use the voucher to send their kid to private school rather than public school. You see, this helps me because the kids can then pay to attend my school, and it helps the parents because it gives them more options, more flexibility, as well as forcing public schools to be more competitive to keep those students and keep those dollars. There's one thing about him, though, that I think may cause problems."

"What's that?"

"Well, . . . oh, we'll have to talk about it later,

30

The Trumpet Is Blown

I see my young prodigy is here," Hassan said, as Jibril rang the doorbell.

David Lamb

Chapter Six

"What's wrong Jibril, you haven't been concentrating all day today? It's not like you to be so distracted. What's up?" a concerned Hassan asked.

"Ah, nothing. Nothing is wrong." Despite the denial, Jibril's voice rang with frustration, and Hassan, with characteristic tender tenacity, pressed him.

"Nah, young blood, I can tell something is wrong, what's up? Talk to me."

"It's just my grandmoms--we had an argument this mornin'." Sucking teeth and rolling eyes confirmed the source of his irritation.

"About what?"

"She still be eatin' swine! And I told her not to be bringin' no pork in the house! It's crazy. Her own doctor already told her she has to stop eating it. I overheard her tell her sister that--and she still won't stop!" Jibril's pouted lips angrily contorted in disgust and piercing eyes burning passionately reminded Hassan of his own youthful zeal.

"Oh, I see, sometimes I forget how abrasive you young brothers can be." His calm, even manner contrasted sharply with Jibril's aggravated tone. "What you've got to understand, young brother, is that teaching is like making great music. You want the tone, the rhythm, the melody of the music to be sweet to the listeners' ears, to touch their hearts, to be so evocative that they can envision what your music is saying, even without a video. If you study it carefully, you'll see that it's the same with the message of the Qur'an. Its tone, rhythm, and melody are sweet to the reader's ear, so that they can hear the truth. It touches the reader's heart so they can feel the truth and its parables are so powerful that one can't help but see the truth. Well, you've got to be the same way. The Qur'an tells us to invite others to Islam 'with wisdom and beautiful preaching: and [to] argue . . . in ways that are best and most gracious.' See, it says 'invite', when you invite someone to something it's not a demand, it's, well, an invitation. Understand? It's like my grandmother always said, 'you can catch more flies with honey than you can with vinegar.' You dig?"

"Yeah, I uh, 'dig', I guess."

"Good."

Hassan had to laugh at Jibril's youthful enthusiasm. His wide-eyed naivety reminded Hassan of himself. Sometimes, talking to Jibril, Hassan would be reminded of the lessons he learned at the feet of his musical forebears.

As a struggling young musician who was happy, grateful, for any gig, Hassan had once been blessed to travel to Tunisia, Algeria, and Turkey on a State Department-sponsored tour.

He had always admired Dizzy Gillespie, and leapt at the chance to travel with his band and learn firsthand from the master. Then when he learned that Art Blakey was going to be part of the band, he simply could not believe his luck.

Once they arrived in Tunisia, the exotic sights and sounds immediately intoxicated Hassan. Blakey, who'd become an Ahmadiyya Muslim years before and had previously played in Tunisia, took him under his wing, guiding him through Tunis, the Tunisian capital. (Dizzy was glad to be rid of Hassan, as the young trumpeter had nearly chewed his ear off on the long plane ride over).

One night, after performing for a packed house, the band shared a meal at a local cafe. The cafe was actually closed, but the owner, who loved Jazz, agreed to let the band in for an after-hours meal. As the evening and the meal progressed, Dizzy, gregarious as ever, invited the owner over and he came and sat. He had a local paper with him that had an article about Malcolm X visiting Egypt, and wanted to know what the band thought of Brother Malcolm.

Before the trip, Hassan had never heard of the Bahai faith, let alone knew that Dizzy was Bahai. And while he had met several musicians who'd converted to Islam, he was only vaguely familiar with the faith, and had no idea that Blakey had converted and taken the name Buhaina.

Throughout the tour, the soaring wail of the muezzin's call to prayer captivated Hassan and left a permanent musical impression on him. (Blakey told him that the best callers came from Senegal, as the Africans had a sentimental attachment to Bilal, the Ethiopian who became the first muezzin in Islamic history.)

Hassan cherished his time abroad. He grew so much as a musician and as a person. He'd keep Dizzy up late into the night discussing one idea after another until finally Dizzy would just roll over and go to sleep on him. Likewise, he'd talk to Blakey until the drummer just tuned him out.

Traveling overseas had challenged some of Hassan's basic notions about music, politics and faith. Yet, while he could understand and respect where Blakey was coming from, there was something about Islam that was alien, foreign to him. He couldn't connect.

Those times had faded into the recesses like ancient, happy memories. Back in the States, he'd been so busy trying to get his career off the ground that he had almost forgotten how much he cherished those late nights in Tunisia chewing Dizzy's and Art's ears off. He was sitting in his living room thinking of those times and wondering how he was going to pay the rent, when he got a call asking him to fill in at a gig at the Hi-Hat Club in Boston playing with Alvan Farrakhan's band. Alvan was a piano player in the Bud Powell be-bop mode. He was also in the Nation of Islam, and like Hassan, Dizzy, and Art, Alvan and Hassan would stay up late into the night talking about the problems of Black people and about the Nation's philosophy. Hassan was already disenchanted with the behavior of white American Christians. He agreed with how Dizzy had put it. When they went down

South to play, they couldn't even worship in the same churches as whites, so like Dizzy said, he didn't feel like he was forsaking Christianity because Christianity had already forsaken him.

While he was in Boston, he went with Alvan to the local Temple to hear what the brothers had to say. He was really taken with the idea of 'doing for self', and they were heavy on that, 'Do For Self'. He could relate to that as a musician, all these black cats creating and playing this beautiful music, but not controlling its production, distribution, and marketing. Sure some of them were getting paid, but they didn't own the companies. And most of them didn't understand the music business, and wound up giving up their publishing rights. One thing Hassan always gave Miles Davis credit for was pulling his coat about music publishing. When Hassan was first coming up, Miles let him sit in on a jam session with him. Hassan was so excited. After they finished, Miles told him that he had nice chops, and gave him some advice on playing and on the business. Hassan never forgot how emphatic Miles was about making sure that he understood how important it was to keep his publishing rights.

After he got back to New York from his Boston gig, he started going to Temple No. 7 up in Harlem, where Louis Farrakhan was the local Minister. Eventually, he joined the Nation and got his X. When Elijah Muhammad died and his son, Warith Deen came in, Hassan saw it as a natural progression, because, he said, Elijah used to tell them that it wasn't his job to teach the religion. He would say that he was trying to clean black people up, and that the one who came after him would teach the religion.

It was in listening to Miles--Sketches of Spain, especially Solea and Saeta--and in talking to Miles that Hassan first began to learn about the music of the Moors. Miles explained how in the Andalusian area of Spain the Moors had a tremendous influence on the whole culture. Miles told him that when he sat down to lay out on Solea and Saeta that he could feel the African rhythm in the trumpets and in the drums; that the modulates and bent notes reminded him of the blues.

While trying to get in on the session where Ole' Coltrane was being recorded, Hassan was reminded of Miles and the Moors. Unfortunately, he wasn't quite able to get his foot in the door. His misfortune turned out to be quite fortuitous, however, because it was there that he met his wife, Khadija. She was trying to get in on the session too, and while neither of them found success, they did find each other.

Years later, when he was preparing to record his own Andalusian-influenced album, Hassan discovered the person who would become his namesake, Abu-l-Hassan 'Ali Ibn Nafi, or simply, Hassan--the most famous singer in Moorish Spain. He was nicknamed Ziryab, the Blackbird--a compliment reflecting his smooth black complexion, eloquent grace with words, and calm, even manner. A brilliant teacher, Ziryab founded the first conservatory of music in Cordova. That's how Hassan came about choosing his name, Hassan Ziryab, 'the beautiful blackbird', because that's what he aspired to be musically. He prayed that one day he would, like the earlier Ziryab, open a full-fledged conservatory, only not in Spain but right in the heart of Bed-Stuy.

The Trumpet Is Blown

Chapter Seven

"Rain, rain go away I need to sell some crack today," Shaun sang playfully as he sought refuge under the used-to-be-white awning of a liquor store. "Damn, it's raining buckets out here today--even the hardcore clientele ain't shown up yet. Yo', Ah'm bouncing," he told J-Son.

"Hold up, we goin' over Mic-Boogie's crib to watch *New Jack City* and play some SuperNintendo."

"Nah, that's ah-ight, I gotta go see my kid."

"Stay real."

"You know that."

Although the downpour had dampened his normal business, Shaun was glad that it had rained. He needed some time to think. He wasn't so sure he could do this anymore. When his son was born, he went into the game to try and make some extra cash before and after school. Before he knew it, the game was starting to take up more time than school, and he couldn't help but see that life on the street wasn't as glamorous as it looks in the movies. He had run into Jibril recently, and he didn't know exactly why, but just seeing that brotha made him feel guilty. He remembered how tight they were coming up, and now to see Jibril making progress, it made him kind of proud. A lot of the brothas thought that Jibril thought that he was all that, but Shaun knew he was cool, he was just taking care of business. Even though they didn't hang anymore, they still spoke whenever they ran into each other, and he knew he had Jibril's back if the shit ever hit the fan; he hoped Jibril had his.

"Psst, yo', yo', Shaun-Love, hook me up, c'mon hook me up, man," a raspy voice cried.

Shaun took one look at Fiend's ragged hide, his filthy T-shirt stained from rain and accumulated dirt, his dirty nails, yellowed teeth, red eyes, unkempt lint-filled head, pockmarked face, and that dumb gap-toothed smile crack fiends put on when they want to put one over. He felt pity, disgust, and shame--all at the same time.

"Yo', Fiend, what you doing out here, man? You ain't even got on no hoodie hard as it's raining out here--you don't even weigh ninety pounds soaking wet. Take your ass inside somewhere and stay dry. And wash up, don't be comin' around here stinkin' no more." It was caring, rational advice, but it was an uncaring, often irrational, business. And Fiend wasn't looking for care. He wanted crack. Badly.

"C'mon man, hook me up, hook me up."

"No, man, look at you, you ain't got no money. No money, no hookup. This is business."

"C'mon man, I got some brand new double A alkaline Everready batteries." Fiend's voice rose with the excitement of a TV pitchman, but Shaun was unimpressed. His frown countering Fiend's yellow grin, he said with deadly seriousness, "Nigga, I don't need no batteries, I need some cash."

"But they brand-new double A alkaline Everready batteries! They keep going, and going and going . . ." Shaun had to laugh at that one.

"Shut up nigga, this ain't no commercial.

The Trumpet Is Blown

Cash, I needs cash," he said, while still laughing.

"All right, then give me a dollar for the batteries."

"A dollar! Boy, iz you crazy?"

"C'mon man, they a dollar ninety-nine in the store," Fiend pleaded pitifully like a tantrum throwing child.

"Let me see 'em," Shaun said, snatching and inspecting the package. "Hmm, they look new. I'll give you fifty cents." After all, his walkman would need batteries soon enough.

"Fifty cents!?" Fiend exclaimed, appalled he was being taken advantage of. After all, that was his job.

"You lucky I didn't say a quarter," Shaun said harshly, snatching Fiend down from his high horse.

"Okay, okay, fifty cents." Fiend acquiesced, meekly holding out his dirt-ladened hand. Shaun dropped two quarters from above, Fiend anxiously caught them and hobbled off.

"Remember, cash nigga, cash!" Shaun yelled as Fiend shuffled away.

There was something almost comical about Fiend's ineptitude. He had tried to be a dealer and wound up getting hooked on the shit himself; now he was one of the worst pookies out there--well most persistent, anyway. (He hadn't yet resorted to some of the foul shit that was driving Shaun away.) He could hardly stomach the thought that he had seen a cracked out brotha offer to give his eleven-year-old daughter to Benjamin Franklin for a night because he

41

didn't have the cash, but he needed the crack, and Benjamin agreed--"cause she had big titties"--and because he liked virgins. Shaun remembered Benjamin laughing about making her bleed. He'd been trying to put it out of his mind, but it was haunting him. He thought about *his* little sister, and knew he'd put someone permanently on their back if they ever even thought about offering her some crack.

The wayward shot careens off the top of the backboard, hops over the fence and runs into the middle of the street. Jibril watches, helpless as a mammoth truck puts an end to the ball's agonizing life. Before he has time to properly mourn the ball's departure, his attention is pulled toward the mass of people running by. Maneuvering his way through the crowd, he's horrified by Marcus' broken body.

Waking up drenched in sweat, Jibril anxiously looks around to see if anyone heard him scream, a technique he'd developed to force himself to wake up. Gathering himself, he wipes his sweat-stained hairline. He sits up in his bed and looks for solace through the window. "Oh good, it's pourin'--that means I don't have to walk past all those knuckleheads today," he thought, while looking out the window at the earth quenching its thirst. "God don't like ugly, so I guess he be using the rain to wash the dirt away," he thought to himself. He and Bilal were supposed to meet Carlos at the Lincoln Center musical library in the City. They planned to listen to some old Jazz tunes, pick up some horn riffs to practice, and some bass riffs to sample. Jibril couldn't wait to hear the <u>Yusef Lateef In Nigeria</u> album that Hassan had turned him on to.

Before he went into the City he had to stop off and pick someone up. It was Saturday, so he had some time to exercise before he left. By the time he got out of the shower he felt immensely refreshed. He hadn't exercised in a long time, and the shower afterwards felt good. His mother and grandmother had gone to the hairdresser, so he had the house to himself, and taking advantage of the solitude he pumped up the volume as he got dressed. He was in a good mood. He turned off the music and picked up the Qur'an, which he had been trying to read straight through, but he kept getting sidetracked. So far he'd read up to the middle of the third chapter. Before he went out, he knew he needed to pray. He'd been slacking off but he was trying to become more diligent. He brushed his teeth, washed his face again, cleaned his ears and nose, rinsed his mouth, wiped his hair and his feet. Then he gathered himself, collected his thoughts, calmed his breathing, and prayed. He felt clean inside and out, with renewed vigor to carry on life's struggles. "Today is going to be a good day," he said to himself, putting his knapsack on and pulling his fitted cap down over his haircut-needing head. He bounded out the door full of positive energy, but before he knew it he was accosted by the foul odor emanating from the apartment two floors down. "Damn, man, we gonna have to call Housing again, those muthufuckin' crackheads! That damn apartment is stinkin', I can't even walk by there without gettin' sick from the funk," he said as he kicked the foul apartment door in frustration, and kept on his way.

Of course, one man's sewage dump was another man's home. For Fiend and his crackhead cohorts, the apartment was just a safe place to smoke and crash in relative peace. Peace? An overstatement, for truly it was a hell hole, seven crackheads in a two-bedroom apartment, nobody working, each fiending for ever more crack. The women were selling whatever they had to get that money. The men used to be squeegee men, but business had dried up ever since the cops started cracking down, driving them from the marketplace; so now they were on shoplifting missions, purse snatching junkets, panhandling parades. Fiend used to be named Curtis, but he'd fallen so low to his addiction that people just started calling him Fiend. He'd inherited the apartment two years earlier from his maternal grandmother after she'd died from a broken heart. Jibril could remember seeing him one day standing in a helpless stupor under the blazing hot sun, thoroughly drenched in sweat and its accompanying foul odor. He'd been up all day and night walking around desperately searching for crack money, and his body had simply given out--he could not move. When Fiend embarked on a mission for crack he lost all sense of time, until reality came crashing on him with podiatric problems that would be hard for the non-crackhead to imagine: bunions, fungi, advanced case athletes' foot, hammer toes, cracked heal calluses, corn muffin-sized corns--podiatric problems.

Emmagene, Fiend's girl, once a beautiful woman, shapely, with large expressive eyes, had come up from North Carolina one summer. When she first arrived, she was as beautiful as the majestically magnificent magnolia grandiflora that first arrived in Bed-Stuy from the same state as Emmagene, as a mere seedling way back in the 1880s. Somehow flourishing in spite of harsh Northern winters, the grand magnolia's beauty has been a natural source of peace, contentment, and contemplation in the midst of concrete sidewalks for generations. Unfortunately, life in the North was not as kind to Emmagene. Caught up by the glitter and glare of New York street life, she fell for Fiend--he still seemed to be the man at that time. She'd never imagined that she would be selling her body to support both their habits. And now she was pregnant!

As crack-addicted as Emmagene was, her addiction paled in comparison to the apartment's other pookies. By far, the most far gone was Grunt. Grunt was what everybody called him; 'Grunt', because he didn't speak in sentences anymore, just unintelligible grunts whose varying tones somehow gave them a ring of intelligibility. He had spent the last three years walking around in slowly disintegrating rags, stinking, his eyes glazed over and vacant. For him, there was no end in sight. Mark was the new kid on the block. Nobody really knew much about him, he'd just had some crack to share, so they let him stay in the apartment too. The other kid didn't even have a name, and nobody was even sure how he was staying there. There was another woman, 'Fly girl', because she used to be a fly girl, metaphorically; now she quite literally was a fly girl, languishing in shit. The last member of this un-magnificent seven was Billy, a white mailman who'd been having an affair with a sista in the projects, and had gotten himself caught up in the crack cycle and lost everything. This coterie of crackheads must have been what Chuck D was talking about when he wrote Night of the Living Baseheads.

"Y-y-y-yo', give me th-th-that lighter muthu . . .," Fiend said, as he snatched the lighter from Grunt, who grunted in response. "Nigga, don't be grunting at me!" Crackheads would do an Ali-Frazier in a minute for a lighter--if you got no heat, no smoke!

Even in the midst of his craving, on occasion, split-second flickering glimmers of clarity would come to Fiend and he'd be forced to question how he was living, particularly ever since Emmagene had reluctantly confided in him that she might be pregnant. He had to make a change. He just couldn't. "Damn," he said, "it's crazy, Emma, it's like, it's, it's, it's like, Ah'm a pookie, but I ain't a pookie! I gotta stop this shit." As he put the pipe to his mouth and flicked the flame he said, "It's fuckin' my life up . . ."

"*We* gotta stop this, Curtis."

"I know, I hate this shit," he said as he passed Emmagene the pipe. "It's crazy, 'cause as much as I hate this, as much as I . . . I, I love this shit at the same time, when you put that fire to those rocks those smoke signals rise through the pipe, and it's like, it's like heaven . . ."

"No Curtis, it's hell, believe me," she said, as she took yet another hit.

"I know but Ah'm addicted to that feelin'."

"Me too, but just as quick as it comes, as soon as you get that feeling, as soon as you get that feeling, it's gone, it's gone, and you chasing that shit again," her glazed, vacant eyes trailed off into some distant space trip. She was thinking about her unborn baby, and couldn't believe that she was putting the deadly pipe to her mouth yet again. "Oh God, make me stop," she silently prayed.

Before he'd cracked up, Fiend had played high school basketball. He was pretty good too, at least that's what everyone says, that he could definitely have played Division I--some say that he may have even made the pros, or at least played in Europe. Who knows?

"I can't believe Ah'm pregnant. I can't believe Ah'm pregnant! I can't believe Ah'm pregnant!" Emmagene thought to herself. "I have to get rid of this baby. I have to."

The Trumpet Is Blown

Chapter Eight

"You know it's funny, I just remembered the first time I heard the word 'Muslim'," Nsinga said with a cute laugh. "To me it sounded like something terrible. I was in the sixth grade, and had on this white skirt with a matching big white shirt, and a brotha at school laughed at me and said that I looked like a 'Muslim'. I didn't even know what a Muslim was, but I said 'I ain't no Muslim', because since he was laughing I figured it had to be something bad."

Jibril liked Nsinga--she always made him laugh. Deep peanut butter brown with sparkling eyes and bubbly cheeks that painted her face in a perpetual smile--she looked like a young, tall, tanned Winnie Mandela. She was the vocalist for their group; she could rap and scat. Sometimes, on the way home from school, they would go down to the Brooklyn Bridge and Jibril would serenade her on the trumpet at the height of the Bridge, while she kicked some funky far out verse. He wanted to take it to the next level but knew she wouldn't go for it. While he wasn't proud of it (outside of machismo male bonding), and knew it wasn't consistent with his Islamic beliefs, he hadn't quite sowed his oats yet, so he kept a certain distance from her. It was something he'd heard her mention once in a thinly-veiled true-to-life criticism, she said: "Muslim guys say they want a Muslim woman, but they're always chasing non-Muslim women because they know that they're loose and they can do things with them." Now, obviously this was a

David Lamb

gross generalization, Jibril thought--both of the
Muslim brothers and of the non-Muslim women. But
even gross exaggerations contain kernels of truth, and
he knew it did, but hey, he figured, "I'll calm down
when I get older." For now they had to finish the
demo for their debut album: <u>Wherever You Go There
You Are</u>.

As Hassan was a mentor for Jibril, Hassan's
wife, Khadija, who was an accomplished flutist in her
own right, mentored Nsinga, who'd come into Khadija
and Hassan's life when they took her in as a foster
child between her sixth and seventh grade. They
hadn't really thought about whether she'd have
negative views of them as Muslims (she did at first,
but more importantly, she was just looking for a family
to love and be loved by).They hadn't really planned on
her conversion, they just knew that anybody they took
in was going to have to live by their household rules,
and if they came to appreciate Islam by the example
they set, then that would be an extra blessing. After
all, they thought, isn't that the way the Qur'an says it's
supposed to be, not by compulsion, but by example
and beautiful preaching?

When Nsinga first moved in, (her name was
Ann then) she didn't quite know what to make of her
foster parents. That first day at their house she was
caught a little off guard when she, in response to
Khadija's asking her what she would like for dinner,
said, "Pork chops." The frown on Khadija's face told
her something was wrong, and Khadija reading Ann's
face, relinquished her frown, and gently explained to

50

her that they didn't eat pork. (Compulsion of belief was one thing, but pork was another.) Nsinga remembered wondering how they could eat pizza if it didn't have sausage and pepperoni on it, but she adjusted. At the foster home there were hardly any books--nevertheless, Ann had always loved to read, so she'd just reread the same books over and over again. At the Ziryabs home, she could take full advantage of the library they'd set up at the end of the basement, and she did. She remembered falling in love with the name Nsinga when she discovered the great African queen and abolitionist, and found that depending on the way it was translated and the way it was pronounced it could actually be 'Ann Zinga'. She liked that. It made a connection for her. Over time, living with the Ziryabs, she came to want to be a full part of their family and to some day have a family of her own like theirs. The first night she spent at her new home, she was awakened early in the morning, frightened by an eerie wail coming from downstairs. At first she didn't know what it was, she just knew she was scared, and got up to investigate. She tiptoed out of her room and gently walked toward the living room following the strange sound, her heart racing with anticipation. She nearly jumped when she saw Hassan. Standing, facing east, with his hands cupped behind his ears, as if to amplify his voice, she could hear what he was saying, but couldn't make it out. It certainly wasn't English. It was some strange language. She didn't know if they were going to make a sacrifice or what. She was ready to get out of that house.

51

However, when she saw Khadija and the boys line up for prayer, and then afterward when they each read a verse from the Qur'an and wished each other well, something struck Ann that dawn. She knew this is how she wanted her family to be.

"Hey, Jibril," Nsinga said suddenly as if a notion had just come to her, "tell me what you think of this, right. I was walking with these girls from school the other day, I was the only one who's Muslim, and we were going to the Fulton Street Mall downtown, right. Now, it's funny we were all together, but the guys in the store when they see me dressed modestly, like a Muslim, they always be addressing me as 'sister', or 'Nubian princess', or 'black woman'. Brothas who aren't even Muslim be given me their best 'as salaam alaikums'. They go out of their way to be nice, almost like Ah'm their mother or something. It's kind of weird because while they're more than ready to step to my girlfriends, they won't even think of stepping to me. It's like I'm untouchable or something."

Jibril was excited as he rode into the City. He was anxious to check out the Mario Bauza albums Carlos had promised to bring. He knew that Bauza had been influenced by Dizzy, and thought that he might be able to pick up some new techniques from him.

"Yo' wussup?" Carlos shouted enthusiastically, his right-hand crashing down against and firmly embracing Jibril's.

"Yo', what up kid. As salaam alaikum." His right-hand rising and slapping solidly against Carlos'.

"Wa alaikum as salaam. Yo', wussup, how's that new piece comin'?"

"It's all that and a bean pie!" He winked at Carlos in between the light rain drops.

"Word?"

"Most definitely."

"Wait hol' up--step back let me see that hat? Oh wow, that's the bomb. Where'd you get that from?" Carlos said, shamelessly admiring Jibril's new baseball cap.

"'Wise Up'," Jibril sniffed loudly, effectively conveying to Carlos his psychic joy that Carlos was sweating his style. "It's this joint in Brooklyn down the block from Spike's. He's got all types of positive message gear in there, but wit' the flava. When I went in there and saw these baseball caps, wit' Al-Islam written across them, wit' the yellow letters on the green, and the yellow bill! Like the A's joints--I had to get one."

"Yeah, that's dope, why didn't you hook me up?"

"Didn't have enough money, kid."

"What, with all that money you makin' as a messenger?" Carlos said sarcastically.

"Yo', you give me the money and next time I'm there I'll pick you up one."

"Okay, bet."

"Yo', where's Bilal?"

David Lamb

"He should be here in a minute. When I went by his house to pick him up, his mom's said that he had to go somewhere, but that he said that he'd meet us here. Oh hold up. I think I see him comin' now under that giant black umbrella."

"Yeah, that's him, don't you see that little extra bop?"

"Oh, yeah, that's him, most definitely. Yo' what up, kid? Peace."

"As salaam alaikum."

"Wa alaikum as salaam, brotha, I thought you wasn't gonna make it." Hand slaps abounded.

"Nah, I'm always on time."

"Yeah, colored people time," Jibril said, with a laugh.

"Where's Nsinga?" Bilal asked.

"Back in Brooklyn, she had to do something for her mom's. Yo' you've got to check this out before we get to the library."

"What?" Bilal asked.

"Yo', last night I saw this crack babe take a leak right in the middle of the block. She just pulled her pants down, right there and took a leak!"

"Get outta here!" Carlos said disbelievingly.

"If Ah'm lyin', Ah'm flyin'," Jibril said, while solemnly holding his left palm over his heart with his right hand upraised as if he were swearing in at the O.J. trial.

"C'mon, man stop, lyin'," Bilal added in disbelief.

"Look I'm tellin' ya'll she took a leak right in

54

the middle of the block!"

"C'mon."

"Just bared her backside and let it ride."

"Damn, what are we comin to?"

"Aw, it wasn't that bad. She did it over the train grate, so at least she was sanitary. She could have done it right in the middle of the block," Jibril said sarcastically. "Yo' sometimes you got to laugh to keep from cryin'."

"Damn, that's messed up!" Bilal said.

"So bust it, Carlos, did you bring those records?" Jibril asked.

"Did *you* bring Miles?" Carlos countered.

"Yeah, I got it."

"Well, give it up."

"Where's yours?"

"Right here."

"Cool, don't let nothing happen to my Miles."

"You just take care of mine."

"C'mon, let's get out of this rain."

"All right, but let's stop in this McDonald's right quick--I got to take a leak," Bilal said.

"Yo' man, you don't need no McDonald's, there's a train grate right there," Jibril said, laughing hysterically.

"Yeah, ah-ight, that was a good one, you got me. Let's go."

"So, Carlos," Jibril said, as they walked through the light mist. "Wussup wit' you and Miles anyway? I thought you just wanted to kick that Latin Jazz."

"Nah, that's not what I said. What I said was David Sanchez's stuff didn't have enough of a Latin flavor for me, I didn't say that's all I wanted to play. We all know Miles was the man."

"I woulda thought you'd be down with Dizzy, since he was on that Cuban style for so long."

"Yeah, Dizzy's cool, but I'm tryin' to get that Miles mood. I think that'll be the move over some hip hop tracks, wit' me kickin' a little Gil Scott Heron-type rhyme."

"Hold up now, stick to the Salsa. Leave Gil Scott alone," a laughing Jibril said.

"Please, I be tellin' people Boricquas was on the set since back in the days--been representin' since Felipe Luciano and the original Last Poets."

"Oh yeah, speakin' of the Old School, that reminds me, yo' bust it right, peep this. Check it out right, I had this crazy, crazy dream about the Furious Five as a Jazz band! I mean they were blowin'--I mean playing for real! It was crazy, Melle Mel was on the sax, Raheem was on trumpet, Flash on drums, Cowboy on Bass, Kid Creole on flute and Scorpio on piano. It was bugged 'cauz they came on stage like they was gonna rap, had on all that gear that they used to wear from yesteryear and then outta nowhere, Melle Mel pulls out a sax, and starts rockin' it, Cowboy dropped that bass, Raheem came in, Flash started droppin' bombs, they was rockin'! Rockin' like Art Blakey and the Jazz Messengers kickin' that hard bop on <u>High Modes</u>. For real. And then it just stopped. The lights went out and I was sittin' in the audience in the dark, wondering how I'd even got there, then one of those bright, twirling disco strobe lights came on and Roxanne Shante was in front of the band dressed like, well, well Roxanne Shante, talkin' like well, well . . . Roxanne Shante. Then the music started real slow and gentle in the background, I didn't know what to expect, and she started singing, beautifully, a la Abbey Lincoln talkin' 'bout Freedom Now, *youknowwwhatahm'sayin'*! And as she sang her appearance transformed, and by the time she was through the crowd didn't know what to do. She looked all regal--like an African queen--*knowwhatImean?* It was quite a scene, I couldn't help but smile, then I heard somebody rappin' turned around and it was Gomer Pyle and I said to myself, *damn*, it's time to wake up now!"

Chapter Nine

"Picture dat, me workin' at Micky D's, nigga please,"Benjamin Franklin boldly bragged as he turned down the sound booming from his new, shiny, black Range Rover. He was talking to his man on the cellular, and his own bass was drowning him out. "I got big plans, nigga, big plans."

"Yo' man, yo', Benjamin?"

"What up Glock?"

"I was just thinkin', you know when was the first time I knew I had to be in the game? Check it, right, I had a crush on that ho', Bali, remember her?"

"Yeah, she was dope."

"Yeah, well her pops used to give me grief and shit, like I wasn't good enough for her, and that nigga was a dope fiend! *Youknowwhatah'msayin'*," Glock said in disbelief at the nerve.

"Here," Benjamin said as he tried to pass Glock the remainder of the long, thick, imported, premium, marijuana-laced Phillie blunt.

"Hold up nigga, let me finish the story. Well, anyway, that nigga owed that kid Priest some heroin money, right, so Priest and those two big niggaz he used to have wit' him all the time rolled up on his monkey ass, fuck'd him up, dragged his ass in front of the buildin' and beat him down--right there in front of everybody! Then Priest jumped on top of his ass, pinned his shoulders under his knees and started beatin' that nigga upside his head wit' his shoe."

"Yeah, that nigga used to wear those hard ass,

The Trumpet Is Blown

shiny, burgundy alligator shoes."

"Yeah, he whooped his monkey ass, his lips were all swoll, busted and bloody, that mu'fucka was screamin' 'I was gonna pay, I was gonna pay!' Like a little bitch! By the time they finished, his eye was all bulgin', swolled shut and shit. And then Priest gets up and wipes the blood off all over that nigga's white shirt! Yo', Priest was mad cool!"

"Yeah, I remember being like in the fifth grade ridin' in the elevator wit' that nigga, and he had a mufuckin' stack of twenties hangin' over his pants, right here, just hangin'. So I told him his money was showin'. He looked down and saw his shirt was rolled up and pulled his shirt down, and then, and then, that nigga gave me a twenty just for lookin' out! And then, and then, to top it off that nigga's bitch was crazy fine," Benjamin said as his voice rose with excitement, while he gave Glock a high five.

"Straight up, she was the bomb. Remember how in the summer, she used to be laid out in front of the buildin' oilin' herself down on that yellow and white lawn chair in that one-piece red body suit gettin' a tan?" Glock gleefully agreed.

"That's when I knew I had to be player. Plus that nigga was always clean! Niggaz nowadays don't know how to dress. Fuck that guerilla look, if Ah'm gettin' paid, Ah'm-a-look like Ah'm gettin' paid, *knowwhatah'msayin'*. See these tailor-mades I got on? Shee-it."

Benjamin Franklin still remembered being called uncle Ben and being teased to no end in junior high, before he left school for good. In the sixth grade his moms was so low on dough that Ben wore knock-off everything, and had to share that with his younger brother--even his underwear and socks were irregulars.

"My education's low, but I got long dough," was his creed. He sang it so often that he probably owed Ice-T royalties.

Benjamin probably would have recorded "Fuck Compton," if Tim Dog hadn't beaten him to it. After all, he was always saying, "I can't stand those L.A. niggaz. They stealin' Brooklyn's props."

Above all, even though he was a dealer, Benjamin hated being treated like a criminal. Whenever he'd go to Macy's to stock up on some new clothes or to buy his girl of the moment some jewelry, he'd be followed, and nothing would make him angrier--except being followed in a Korean owned store. "Word, I hate them Korean mu'fuckas, every time you roll in one of they stores, they tryin'na creep. Like Ah'm a steal sumptin' as much money as Ah'm makin', *youknowwhatah'msayin'*," Glock growled with a gold-ladened frown. "Fuck dem niggaz!" he exclaimed, as Benjamin nodded his head vigorously in agreement.

Jibril felt the same anger Benjamin felt. Every time he went to school, the ubiquitous amenities of the Upper West Side reminded him of the dearth of stores on his side of town. Every time he wanted to buy

The Trumpet Is Blown

some jeans, a clerk followed behind. Sometimes he felt like stealing a pair just because they'd dared to treat him so unfair. Every now and again he wondered if it wasn't for the trumpet, if he too might've just said 'fuck it!'

When they were kids, Jibril would play touch football with Benjamin and Shaun and a whole gang of little rascals. Fiend was still Curtis then, he was a San Francisco Forty-Niner fan; being about six years older than the rest he'd play coach, designing plays and assigning positions. It would be Shaun and Jibril's building versus another building or group of buildings. One day, while going deep a la Jerry Rice, Jibril was distracted by Landa's laughter as she played double Dutch in front of her building about twenty yards from the football game. Landa was the prettiest girl in the neighborhood. She rendered all the little boys helpless. Still running, but helplessly looking at Landa, Jibril accidently crashed into a sprinting Benjamin, who, protecting himself from the impending tumble, thrust his hands forward to cushion the pain of the fall. Having skidded along the dry, rough dirt, burning and scraping his hands, Benjamin got up swinging. Jibril was caught off guard. After all, it wasn't intentional. Benjamin punched him square in the mouth with a swift, hard right hand, drawing blood. Curtis quickly jumped in and broke the combatants up. That would've been the end of it, but as it happened Marcus was walking by. Seeing his brother's bloody mouth, he ordered him back into the ring. Jibril knew that if he didn't fight, he'd have to

David Lamb

answer to Marcus later. It didn't matter if he won or
lost--just that he fought.

The Trumpet Is Blown

Chapter Ten

Pop, pop, pop went the nine. Pop, pop, pop . . . pop, pop, pop . . . pop, pop, pop went . . . pop, pop, pop went the nine--with the pow pow boogie and the Big BANG! BANG! Welcome to the Terrordome.

Just a little over an hour before, the popping sound of erratic gunfire echoing through the night had blasted holes in Jibril's concentration.

The first time Jibril could remember hearing gunshots was in the seventh grade, the spring before his brother died. He was at a block party when an argument broke out somewhere in the crowd. At first he just heard loud voices against the music, but then he heard a piercing scream, then a shot, then another shot, and saw everyone run for cover. It was a wonder he wasn't run over. He didn't run with the others, he just stood next to a tree and watched the pandemonium.

The second time he heard shots was during the summer basketball league. Some of the players from one of the losing teams thought they'd been shown up, and came back firing not jumpshots, but buckshots at the star player on Jibril's team. The young brotha ran and leaped over the fence in a desperate attempt to get away, but not before he took two shots where it would be difficult for him to sit for a while.

The next time he heard gunshots he didn't just hear them--he saw the spark of the shot, and the damage inflicted. He was sitting with Bilal (who was then Carl) at the handball court where they were shamelessly admiring the sistas. They were in the ninth grade and Carl had on some very brand new Air Jordans, crisp and spanking white, with MJ's silky silhouette sparkling under the bright sunlight, looking as though he were leaping off the sneaker itself. Carl had bought them from money he'd saved working at McDonalds.

With his new Jordans on, Carl thought--no, knew--he was the man. Chris saw him checking out Shonice walking over from the handball court. Carl was damn near licking his lips, and Chris knew he had found Carl's motivation. There they sat, as Heavy D pumped from a parked blue Nissan. Carl posed with a bottle of Guiness Stout in a sufficiently crinkled brown bag, pulled down just enough to reveal the very tip top of the bottle, cocked in his hand, tilted up like a ripely aged quart of Ol' E. The broad smile on Carl's face as he was talking to Shonice damn near blinded Chris, which inspired him to lean over and quietly ask,

"Yo', are you cold, and shit?"

"It's 70 degrees out here, Negro, how Ah'm a be cold?"

"Well, if you ain't cold, why you wearin' that yellow coat on your teeth?" Chris whispered out of the corner of his mouth, turning only his eyes toward Carl.

"Man, you just wish you was in my shoes right now."

Handball courts in the springtime could be interesting places. From the palm striking the ball, the

The Trumpet Is Blown

ball striking the wall, the cement striking the ball and the ball being struck by the palm anew, the cycle continues in a rhythmic fashion syncopated to multitudinous beats booming from passing cars. Strikingly-fine sistas with gazelle-like grace, leaving brothas dazed as they bend and twist with athletic flair and sublime beauty. Brothas customarily talking shit with so much enthusiasm that one had to wonder what was more fun, playing or talking shit. With all that activity comes a certain amount of noise, so when things suddenly get quiet, the silence is, so to speak, deafening.

When the sound of a bottle top crashing mightily against the pavement startled Chris, snapping him out of his musically-induced trance, it was only natural that he wonder aloud, "Why is everything so quiet all of a sudden?" With profound resignation, Carl pointed toward the handball court with his chin. Approaching them purposefully and menacingly were four brothas Chris had not seen before. The first, the third, and the fourth had guns drawn. The first kid had on a pair of all white Nikes, faded jeans and most important, a silver Berretta. He strolled by slowly, and turned to his right with military precision, cocked his gun, waving it slowly and deliberately past Chris' face, and continued on past Shonice's--stopping momentarily to wink at her, an impish grin revealing gold and missing teeth--and then moved on, putting his gun on Carl's cheek. "Don't do anything stupid, kid. Just give up the Jordans." Carl took a deep breath. He wanted to shake his head, but he just stared at the kid, and then started untying his Nikes, cursing under his breath.

"What you say, nigga?" The gun was now perilously close to Carl's head, as he glanced up it seemed as though his eyes were trapped inside its barrel.

"Nothing, I ain't say nothing."

"Oh, I thought so, mutha . . ., hurry the fuck up. Hey, yo' what the fu___?! Don't scuff up my sneakers, or Ah'm-a-have-to-bust-a-cap-in-yo'-punk-ass."

The second kid following closely behind, walked by, took the Jordans (luckily Carl had on new socks), and kept walking toward a car parked on the corner. The first kid started to walk off, as the last two kids walked up guns drawn, looking like they were auditioning for a video. As they backed away, the last kid put his gun on Carl's nose and pushed it up, laughing, then as he backed away he pointed it at Chris, and suddenly fired--into the ground. Although he managed to look back at the kid defiantly, the lump in Chris' throat nearly choked him, but he was luckier than Shonice. A piece of shrapnel ricocheted off the concrete ripping into her calf causing her to scream in horror as blood began rapidly gushing from her lower left leg. At the sight of the profusely-streaming blood, the gunman was momentarily dumbstruck, as his equally-startled boys grabbed him and they ran off to the car together. Until then, Jibril had never actually seen anyone die from being shot. At first he didn't even realize she'd been hit, the gun had been fired into the ground, after all. But then she screamed, a terrible scream, so visceral that it seemed as though the very ground screamed. And the blood, all that blood, just kept gushing. He tried desperately to stop the flow by clamping the wound with his hands, but they just kept getting bloodier and bloodier, like Macbeth's. He finally managed to snap Carl out of his stupor, and got him to run for help. By now a crowd was gathered, frantically yelling incomprehensible instructions. Jibril looked on in terror as he saw Shonice's eyes roll. He screamed in vain for her to hold on.

David Lamb

Chapter Eleven

Under a picture of Malcolm X shaking hands with Adam Clayton Powell, and to the tune of Marvin Gaye asking "What's Goin' On?", Benjamin carried on three conversations simultaneously, one with his barber whom he barked instructions at, one with a girl on his ever-present cellular, and one with Glock who was proudly getting his nails manicured by a nervous salt and pepper-haired slightly plump elderly woman trying to make a little extra cash on the weekends. As Jibril sat down to get his hair cut, a fifty-year-old teenager came in wearing the same loose-fitting jeans Jibril saw him in the last time he'd gotten his hair cut. "A one is leading," the would-be hip hopper announced to the shop. "Damn, I knew I should've played a one."

It was all so familiar, Jibril could always count on his barber's reply, whatever number the Redd Foxx-favoring teenager said was leading, his barber would reply, "Damn, I knew I should've played a . . ." Jibril chuckled at the thought, happily sharing a secret laugh with Kevin, the talkative young brotha who worked at the barber shop after school, sweeping up and wiping hair off of customers' clothing eager to earn a little spending money. Jibril always tried to give him an encouraging word along with a tip, just to encourage him to stay in the legal economy. "Give me three ones--and combinate it," Glock said confidently, whipping out a rubber band roll of fives and ones. It was a good thing he had his money out, because just as he was placing his bet, a brotha came in peddling new Nike pullover rain jackets. Jibril was always amazed at how many roles your average barber shop played. On the one hand, you went there to get a haircut, on the other, you could always count on someone coming in peddling wares. Just that day, an older female pookie had come in peddling stolen steak knives, an older brotha had come in peddling vitamin C pills he'd boosted from a health food spot, and now this brotha had come in with the Nike jackets. Jibril had to admit they were nice--navy blue, with a wine-colored raised stitch line going across the middle splitting it in two, and above the stitched line, the word 'Nike' was spelled out in big italicized letters. And it had a tuckable hood. It was really very nice. "How much?" he asked.

"Twenty," the brotha eagerly replied, happy at the thought of a sale. Jibril wanted one, but he was a little short, and had to pass. "Yo', yo' let me check it out," Benjamin said waving the traveling salesman over. "Yo' Glock, bust it," he said as he flung a jacket in Glock's direction.

"Yo' these is dope," Glock confirmed.

"Give me two," Benjamin bragged, now whipping out *his* stack of freshly-ironed, formerly-wrinkled bills. (Benjamin didn't play when it came to his money, it had to look a certain way--he detested the filthy, crumpled bills the pookies paid with and he had the dirty bills washed, and paid a pookie to press them--and they had better be starched!) Kevin's childlike eyes looked longingly at the jackets wishing that he too could have one; Benjamin winked confidently at him and told the salesman to let him get three for fifty. After briefly thinking it over, he agreed. Benjamin called Kevin over and gave him the jacket. Jibril wanted to tell Kevin to give it back, knowing the road this was leading down (remembering Priest giving him and his friends money for performing menial tasks for him when he was a little boy), but he kept quiet. Benjamin glared at Jibril and asked sarcastically if he wanted a jacket too. "Nah, Ah'm cool," he replied stoically. He knew that Benjamin was trying to play him for a chump, but before he could think of a snappy retort, his thoughts were interrupted by a sudden burst of gunfire, as his barber dove to the floor leaving one side of Jibril's head undone. Jibril whirled to see what was happening. He heard another shot and decided to dive to the floor himself. He was frightened by the crashing thud of the water cooler bursting against the floor. The rush of water passed him; he watched in horror as it gradually changed into a crimson tide. The barrage of shots suddenly came to a halt. When he looked up he saw Benjamin and Glock race outside, guns drawn, yelling retaliatory threats. Glancing back behind him, he saw Kevin smiling--blood gushing from his throat. Jibril raced over, trying desperately to dam the flow. The rushing blood soaked through his hands, splattering his clothing. Kevin died in his arms that day, clutching a new Nike jacket.

Jibril's playing had suffered greatly after

The Trumpet Is Blown

Shonice died in his arms like that. His ability to concentrate and compose had been severely damaged by the memory of her last faint breath fading away softly like the concluding note of a gentle ballad. He didn't play for a long time after that.

It was Coltrane and his yoga regimen that resurrected Jibril's creative energies, reminding him of why he played--why he *had* to play.

For Jibril, Kevin's death was an aborted concerto--tyrannical rulers muting the young brotha's voice before the first note was even played.

With his trumpet in hand resting against his right cheek, occasionally tapping the cheek, his back resting against his bed, Jibril stared at the ceiling waiting for the notes to come. None did. He strained, and still none did. It was very late and the pull of sleep left him almost delirious. He glanced at his hands still sticky with Kevin's blood, his hooded sweatshirt now a crimson-tinged blue. His eyes blinked, demanding to be shut, but he refused to honor their request. Slowly, against his will, he began losing consciousness. The ceiling began rotating and bright starlike spots sparkled above. He smiled at the apparent beauty of the night sky. Slowly, it seemed that a human form began to take shape above him gliding among the stars. He squinted to capture the image rapidly approaching, rushing toward him, a horrifying scream rising as the body descends.

David Lamb

It's Marcus.
     Crashing
          right
             into
                him.

Waking up drenched in sweat, Jibril looks around to
see if anyone heard him scream. Gathering himself, he
wipes his sweat-stained brow, as he sits up in his bed
and looks out the window for solace.

The Trumpet Is Blown

Chapter Twelve

"Yo', yo' check it out, we gonna use that Coltrane lick," Carlos said, while flicking through Bilal's extensive vinyl collection, which was strategically organized in old milk crates in alphabetical order according to artist and type of music--Hip Hop, R&B, Jazz, and some Reggae with a little Salsa and some Merengue sprinkled throughout.

"What lick?"

"That Coltrane lick, yeah you know, that one from <u>Syeeda's Song Flute,</u>" Jibril further explained to Bilal.

"Oh yeah! Oh yeah, dat's la bomba, I had just timed that out the other day," Bilal said as he flipped through a pile of albums perched against his speaker searching for the Coltrane cut. "You know it's almost exactly as long as the Sonny Rollins lick Digable used on <u>Time&Space.</u>"

"I know, I know, that's how I know it's gonna work," Jibril pointed out.

"Cool. Yo' Jibril, did you check that Lonnie Liston Smith album I gave you?" Bilal asked.

"What?"

"Yeah, you know, the album Stetsasonic got that bass riff from for <u>Talkin' All That Jazz.</u>" Carlos reminded Jibril by humming his rendition of the tune while looking at the framed picture of the cover from the <u>Freedom Now Suite</u> Bilal had hanging over his bed.

"Oh, yeah, you right. Nah, I haven't listened to it yet."

"One more thing. Have you figured out whose version of Night In Tunisia Gang Starr sampled for Manifest yet?" Bilal was eager to know.

"Nah, I'm still tryin' to figure out how they came up wit' that, 'cauz every version I've heard goes so fast, I didn't even pick out how dope the piano was, but they hooked it up, I got's to give them credit. And JazzThing was in there too, I can't front."

"So, what about that other joint, have you decided yet?" Carlos asked anxiously.

"Yep," Bilal replied with a broad self-satisfied grin.

"Well?" Jibril asked impatiently, his tightly twirling left hand telling Bilal to hurry it up.

"Well I know ya'll gonna think Ah'm buggin' but check it--boop budooh dooh doop/ doo doo doop budooh doo doop doo doo doop budooh doo doop/ doo doo doop budooh doo doop . . ."

"Look, don't be tryin'na hum no beats! I don't understand you Bilal, how you gonna be a D.J. *and* a drummer and you *still* can't hum no beats?" Jibril asked with a chuckle.

"Look, it's not my hummin', it's your hearing. It's Earth, Wind & Fire--That's the Way of the World."

"Earth, Wind & Fire?!"

"Yes Negro! That's right Earth, Wind & Fire. Shit, Ice Cube used Devotion when he hooked up You Can't Play With My Yo Yo for Yo Yo."

The Trumpet Is Blown

"Yeah, you right, you right. I'd forgot about that."

"Here listen to the bass line," Bilal said as he carefully blew along the album, blowing away any dust and gently laying it on his lone turntable. He had to be extra careful taking care of the tools of the trade. He didn't have any extra money to replace ruined vinyls, and on top of that his other turntable had broken months before and he still hadn't been able to get it fixed. So he had to take extra special care to make sure that the working turntable stayed that way, working. "It comes in about ten seconds in," he was excited about his discovery. "Boop budooh dooh doop/ doo doo doop budooh doo doop/ doo doo doop budooh doo doop/ doo doo doop budooh doo doop."

"Ah-ight, ah-ight . . ."

"But you know what's really the bomb about it?" Bilal asked excitedly. "What's really the bomb is we don't have to sample it, we'll just play it over at the studio, so we don't have to worry about gettin' no clearance, *youknowwhatah'msayin'*. Check it, I can play the bassline over on the keyboard, we'll speed it up a little, then you could play that light trumpet lick on top of it, just like on the original, and maybe even bring it out a little more. Then we add that phat drumline underneath that I let you check out the other day . . ."

"Yeah, yeah . . ."

" . . . and we be in business."

"That sounds good, only thing now we got to get studio money," Jibril said soberly, gazing out the

75

window at a squirrel artfully dodging a puppy's
clumsy attempt to chase it down.

"No problem," a smiling Carlos said
confidently.

"What you talkin' bout Carlos?" Bilal asked in
his patented Gary Coleman style.

"Yo', I got us a gig."

"For real, doin' what? I know you. You'll
have us out playin' at some wrestling match or
something."

"Nah, Bilal this is on the up and up."

"Well, doin' what?" Bilal repeated.

"We're goin' to play at this Cuban weddin'."

"Yo', yo' chill, man, I mean Salsa is cool and
all, but I don't know if Ah'm ready to play at no
weddin'," Jibril said.

"Word," Bilal seconded.

"Yo', Jibril haven't you been listening to those
Mario Bauza tapes I let you borrow?"

"Yeah, but . . ."

"Yo', butts are for cigarettes."

David Lamb

Chapter Thirteen

At first Jibril had a hard time understanding what Selim was saying. Jibril was sitting on the train talking to Bilal about the sudden re-emergence of his nightmares. After Marcus died, Jibril couldn't make it through the night without being awakened in a cold sweat by the horrifying recreation of his brother's fateful fall. He would awaken with his mother lovingly caressing his head promising that everything would be all right. Eventually the nightmares subsided, but recently they had started disturbing and penetrating his otherwise peaceful slumber, yet again. The very fact that he would even discuss it with Bilal, instead of keeping it to himself (his mother didn't even know) was a measure of the depth of his concern. Now, his mind was blocked again. He couldn't play. And Hassan was pressing him, anxious to get Jibril into the studio to record some his playing, so that he could hurry up and send it off to Betty Carter (Jibril didn't know, but Hassan had already promised her a tape). And Jibril had been stalling, unwilling to tell Hassan, unwilling to tell anyone about the dreams, about his creative block. Before he and Bilal could really get into it, however, Jibril thought that he'd heard someone say, "What's up sheik?" But he didn't understand why anyone would be calling him 'sheik'. And with Selim Sivad's incredible, ridiculous, phony, exaggerated Arabic accent (he truly didn't know any Arabic, and Jibril could've sworn he'd just converted a couple of months before), it was hard to tell just

78

exactly what he was saying. When Jibril turned to see who was speaking, he, anticipating a confrontation, just wanted Selim to disappear. As far as Jibril was concerned, Selim had been a knucklehead and a bully since at least the second grade (although, unfortunately for Selim, he'd stopped growing by the end of the seventh), and now that Selim had converted it seemed to Jibril that Selim was all turned around, more interested in being an Arab than in being a Muslim.

"As salaam alaikum," Selim said as small drops of soaring saliva splashed Jibril annoyingly across the face.

"Wa alaikum as salaam. Yo' dude, chill with the shower all right," Jibril said with a hint of anger as he wiped his hand across his face.

"Pardon me."

"Yo', how much you sellin' those oils for?" Bilal asked, pointing with his chin to Selim's black knapsack which was practically overflowing with oils and incense.

As Selim turned to respond to Bilal, he noticed the small red, yellow, and green button with the outline of the African continent attached to Bilal's knapsack. Pointing to the button Selim immediately began his tirade, "I don't really identify with that, that's just a game these Europeans run to keep us away from our real history," Selim said arrogantly, emphatically. "They want us to identify with West Africa, because of its low level of civilization, the truth is that there were two different kinds of Africans. The

'Northeast African Arabian'-- who we come from, and the 'West Coastline African', who they want us to say we come from--but we didn't. We came from the Arabian Africans." The more Selim spoke, the angrier Jibril got.

"You know, Selim, not to break, but that shit is stupid."

"No, it's true Jibril, you can tell not only by our features, but by our intelligence that we're from the Arabian Africans."

"I hate to be the one to break it to you brotha, but they could drop you in the middle of Ghana, and nobody would know the difference."

"Word," Bilal added, as he and Jibril shared a laugh and a pound.

"You guys just don't want to face it, ya'll all twisted with that Afrocentric stuff. Look, I can prove it, the 'West Coastline Africans' practiced animalism, cannibalism, and idolatry. If the slaves came from West Africa how come there's no evidence that they ever made idols or practiced cannibalism?"

"Look, first of all I'm not conceding this cannibalism point, but the truth is that there is some evidence of the slaves practicing traditional African religions. I mean, we know there were Muslims who were brought over too, but you can't say that they all were Muslims. You know, Selim, you need to decide whether you tryin' to be a Muslim or an Arab." Just then, the train came to a screeching unscheduled halt the force of which caused Jibril's trumpet case to fly out of its seat and on to the floor.

The Trumpet Is Blown

"Is that your trumpet?" Selim asked arrogantly, his bottom lip contorted in self-righteous satisfaction.

"You know, you really shouldn't be playing no musical instruments. The Qur'an forbids music," Selim said smugly, his self-righteousness growing more apparent.

"Where do you get that from?" Jibril said dismissively.

"I don't know where exactly, but I know it says something about frivolous talk. Listen to these songs, it's beyond frivolous."

"So, let me get this straight, you're saying that because frivolous talk is criticized, that means that music is forbidden?"

"Yep."

"Well, I'm glad that you're not the ultimate judge with that kind of weak reasoning. First of all, music in and of itself doesn't involve lyrics. In fact, if you'd ever studied music, or really knew anything about music, then you'd know that it is a science, the science of sound. And if you have a problem with some lyrics, then your argument is with the content--not the form. Just because some lyrics are offensive that don't mean that lyrics by definition are offensive."

"Well this is my stop." He got no response from either Jibril or Bilal.

"Brothas are always tryin' to make something up," Bilal said as Selim disappeared down the subway steps.

"I know what you mean, man, especially if

there's a crowd."

". . . especially if there are girls in the crowd," Bilal added knowingly. If there was one thing Jibril hated, it was standing on corners holding three hour debates about the most esoteric of topics. It wasn't so much that he didn't like debates, but that debating was all some brothas seemed to do. They never did anything else--no organizing, petitioning, or educating, just standing around waiting to point out the slightest imperfection in others, making up their own prohibitions.

As the train rolled out of the station, Jibril sat down and closed his eyes. He recalled Hassan telling him that he had gone through similar debates in his early days of playing, and how he had found solace in the Qur'an's critique of self-imposed prohibitions when Allah says, "utter not, for what your tongues describe, the lie: This is lawful and this is unlawful; so that you forge a lie against Allah. Surely those who forge a lie against Allah will not prosper."

He breathed deeply, tuning the roar of the train out as he meditated on the liner notes from <u>Peace & Harmony</u>, one of Hassan's earlier albums (and Jibril's favorite). He had framed the notes on the wall in his room. It helped him focus on his musical goals.

DEAR LISTENER: During the recording of this album, I was blessed to discover a wonderful parallel between Jazz and Islam. Both are concerned with peace and harmony, seeking to bring the listener more in tune with the universal order. One day while

The Trumpet Is Blown

rehearsing in the studio, I was struck by the fact that when Muslims greet each other we say, 'As salaam alaikum', and respond 'wa alaikum as salaam'. Peace be unto you, and unto you be peace. This is the expression of the hope for harmonious relations. In the same way, I saw Jazz musicians search for harmony, for notes and chords that when played together produce a pleasing sound.

I realized that just as music is a language of notes and signs, Allah often speaks to us in the Qur'an through illustrative signs by noting or pointing out in nature spiritual lessons behind physical phenomena. This is why its verses, I realized, are known as ayats. Ayat means a sign, because each verse is, as it were, a sign of Allah's mercy and beneficence.

I slowly became aware that just as spiritual messengers are raised to show us the beauty and majesty of creation, to inspire us, to encourage us, and even to reprimand us in order to lead us on the straight path, so too in Jazz are musical messengers raised, who influence the music to a certain point, and then another comes and takes it further or reveals a new way of looking at it. What is more appropriate, I learned, than a musician being in tune with creation? This is why the great musicians who play what has never been played before recognize the need for divine inspiration; recognize that music can itself be a form of worship, a prayer, which if listened to can elevate our understanding and appreciation of prayer's spiritual dimension. These inspired musicians, like the late, great John Coltrane, pray for the gift of revelation, humbly beseeching the Most High to grant them the means and the privilege to make others happy through their playing.

Dear listener, we humbly beseech you to listen to the message of the musicians gathered on this album, representing different eras, cultures, and temperaments. Listen as they interpret <u>A Night In Tunisia</u> each offering their own interpretation, teaching us, as the Qur'an tells us, that among Allah's signs is the diversity of our colors and our tongues, and that each of us, wherever we may be from, whatever language we may speak, has some jewel, some wisdom, some new insight to offer. 'Surely there are signs in this for the learned.'

The Trumpet Is Blown

You always say,
"Don't tell me,
I have eyes,
I can see,"
and I think
to myself
tis' true you have eyes,
but I never saw you see

Chapter Fourteen

"Yo' Benjamin, this old Muslim nigga tried to roll in the building today," J-Son relayed excitedly. "He claimed he was going to buy it from the City or something."

"Oh yeah, so what did you tell him?" Benjamin deadpanned.

"Yo' I told that nigga, the City ain't had no right to sell it 'cauz they didn't own it--we did," a grinning J-Son replied, eager to please his boss.

"Hah, that's good. I can't stand those bean pie-eatin' muthufuckas, they always fuckin' up business. They unreasonable. One of the old heads who put me down wit' the game told me that he had this spot in Queens, in Jamaica, when some Muslims moved in. They had built a church a couple of buildings down, and they had bought the building he was operating out of. He tried to be reasonable wit' them muthufuckas, you know, he offered to pay them rent, or what have you, you know, for lettin' him use the building. He was tryin' to be fair, but they wouldn't even go for that! So we ain't even gonna play wit' him. Next time he comes around, give that ass a good thrashing. Ah-ight?"

"You the man."

"Ah-ight. So, how's business going today?"

"It's ah-ight."

"You sure, it seems like shit is a little slow to me," he said, pressing J-Son for the truth.

"Well, you know," J-Son started hesitantly,

carefully choosing the words from his limited vocabulary. "Shit's been a little slow, all this damn rain, and ever since them Jamaican niggaz opened up that other spot shit has fell off a little."

"Yeah, that's what I thought, 'cause the money's been comin' up a little light. I'm thinkin' we might have to cut the price, cut the product, I don't know though 'cause pookies could tell when you cut the product and they don't like that shit and might take they business somewhere else . . ."

"Like to them Jamaican niggaz . . ."

"Yeah," Benjamin said with a stern glance revealing his annoyance at being interrupted in mid-thought. J-Son lowered his head slightly, and his eyes he lowered a little more, just enough to show contrition. "Anyway," Benjamin continued, "I might have to cut some niggaz loose, but I'm tryin' not to do that, so I might have to cut niggaz back to seventy-five cents a vial. What do you think?"

J-Son knew to tread carefully. Technically, he was the manager of the Lab, but when Benjamin asked his opinion he knew that he generally had already made up his mind. He just wanted verbal agreement. Well, not exactly agreement, more like slightly vague confirmation. Knowing this, J-Son said, "You got to do what you gotta do."

"Yeah, I'll see. I might replace some of them wit' some pookies, 'cause them, I could just pay them with crack, but then I gotta watch them for stealing, so I don't know. Ah-ight, later." J-Son was relieved. "Oh yeah." Too soon. Benjamin continued. "Damn,"

J-Son thought. "Yo' what's up wit' that nigga Beast?"

"Damn!" J-Son thought again. "He aw-ight, he's jus' a little wild sometimes," he said.

"Yo' you gonna have to make sure that nigga chill. I hired him on your word, and that nigga is costing me money wit' dumb shit, beatin' up pookies for laughs. What kinda shit is that? He's costing me bail money. You best to tell that nigga to straighten up or Ah'm a have to dock you, ah'ight," he said peering at J-Son with deadly seriousness.

J-Son glanced over Benjamin's shoulder at a stern-faced Glock standing with his arms folded, right over left, chewing on his ever-present toothpick bobbing his head to the beat blasting from Benjamin's jeep, "All right, Ah'm a make him chill," J-Son said nervously.

"You better."

The Trumpet Is Blown

Chapter Fifteen

While Jibril had to admit that it was beautifully drawn, there was something about the sketch as a whole that was--he tried searching for another word but he couldn't come up with one; there was something about it that was repulsive: A giant white owl perched on top of a boom box radio wearing Adidas with a small gold chain around its neck in the shape of a Nine. In front of the radio to the right of the owl lays an empty bottle of Old English malt liquor, cap off and discarded a few inches to the left of the bottle. In the background of the whole picture, almost silhouette-like, the outline of the head of a ferocious pit bull. What was Nsinga thinking? He wondered to himself. All he had wanted to do was enjoy his lunch of butter cookies and apple juice, and now he had to deal with this. What could he say?

"Gee, I don't know Nsinga, I mean, like, like . . ." Blinking eyes revealed his apprehension.

"Like what?" she said, twisting her lips, slightly impatient with Jibril's fumbling.

"He means it looks kind of repulsive," Bilal responded impulsively, drawing a look from Jibril's darting eyes which said, "Why'd you say that?"

"Is that what you mean?" she asked, sounding a little hurt, the sparkle in her dark brown eyes slightly dampened.

"Well, I . . . I . . . I wouldn't say repulsive . . . that's a little strong."

"Just a little?" she pushed.

"Well . . .," was all he could manage to fumble out before Nsinga said, "Good, at least one of you's not chicken. Thanks Bilal, I wanted it to be repulsive."

"You're welcome," Bilal said smiling, a little surprised, as Nsinga's lips reformed into a mischievous grin and the sparkle returned to her eyes.

"See, that's the whole point. It's like a figurative representation of how hip hop's fallen off in a repulsive kind of way." She was moving her right hand in a slow circular fashion as she spoke, trying to magically pull comprehension out of the boys. "I call it 'Idle Worship', an obvious play on words, I know, thank you," she said laughing. "See, I took some of the tools of idle time brothas be worshippin' and put them all together. The white owl's for the cigars they be usin' to roll their blunts, and see, he's got a chain in the form of a nine around his neck, I mean for real," she said sarcastically, twisting her mouth in mock seriousness, "what gangsta album would be complete without at least a couple of references to Nines. Can't you just hear him sayin'--'My Adidas!' she laughed. "See his eyes are a little red from the Ol' E he's been drinking while listening to these new kids - D.G.A.F."

"D.G.A.F.?" Jibril and Bilal asked simultaneously.

"Yeah, D.G.A.F.," she laughed. "Don't Give A ____. And then, see, behind everything is a giant pit bull watching the owl's back."

"You know Nsinga sometimes I think that

you're really mentally disturbed," Jibril laughed.

"Thank you," she laughed.

"Yo' Jibril, after school let's go to the arcade --I wanna play that new game where you sit down in the car, and it shakes when you crash!" Bilal said enthusiastically.

"Sorry no can do, buckaroo, I got's to go to work today."

"Oh yeah, that's right, my bad."

Jibril couldn't wait to get home and get out of the wet clothes he had on. Those damn sunshine-promising weather forecasters had once again done him wrong. If he had known it was going to rain he would have dressed differently, at least packed an umbrella in his knapsack; especially since he knew he was going to be carrying packages all over Manhattan.

Traveling throughout the City, Jibril found that there was always room for excitement of one kind or another. Sometimes riding the train he felt like a cowboy in the Old West--gunslingers, townspeople, sheriffs, vigilante posses, it was all there. Still in all, even with its Wild West flavor, the term 'iron horse' always seemed like a misnomer to him. After all, you had to get inside the train in order to ride. If you actually tried to ride it like a horse he didn't see how it could work. To him, it was more like Jonah and the whale, because it was almost other worldly to ponder the wide variety of misadventures, mishaps, and miscellaneous mysteries he'd see just sitting there

David Lamb

chilling out.

Wiping the watery edges from around his rain-soaked head, Jibril kicked his head back and laid his trumpet case on his lap, grateful to be out of the storm and happy to have found a seat. He was just starting to lift his headphones from around his neck to his ears, when he heard a young urban cowboy say, "Yo', look at that nigga, kid."

As soon as he heard that, Jibril knew that he was not going to be able to just 'chill out' on this day's train ride. He had to put his game face on.

"Oh shit," the young cowboy's sidekick laughed, "That nigga got a suitcase. Yo' what's in the case, money? Your racing car set?" They both howled at that, as Jibril tried to ignore them.

"Yo', he tryin' to ig' you. What's up wit' that?" the first instigator instigated.

"Yo' you tryin' to ig' me, nigga? I know you not tryin' to dis me, right? Right?"

"Nah, he ain't tryin' to dis you," the first instigator drew back playing good cop. "Yo' what's in the case, G?"

"Okay there are two of them," Jibril thought. "I'll kick that first kid in his . . ."

"Yo' what's in the case nigga?"

"Then I'll crash that other kid with the case," he strategized.

"Yo' what's in the case nigga? Let us check it out, we ain't gonna take it." The second instigator said, trying and failing to sound convincing. Jibril knew that if he opened the case and they took out the trumpet that that would be it, he may as well kiss her goodbye.

"Yo', let me see the case," the first one said in a menacing tone, deepening the bass in his voice as he reached for the case testing Jibril's resolve. "What nigga?!" He said threateningly as he advanced aggressively. Jibril sprang from his seat as the frightened passengers scattered to the far ends of the litter-strewn subway car, knocking each other over in their mad scramble for safety--an old woman ran over a little girl, an old man was motored down by a young man, a preppie-looking white guy lost his glasses as he frantically sprinted from his seat.

"What up, nigga?" Jibril was partly encircled by the two, his back protected by a row of seats. "What up nigga?" The first one asked as he whipped out a box cutter knife. Fear cut across Jibril's face, he could see that it turned the knife wielder on, he had to be sure to block the knife thrust with the case, and then stomp the kid out immediately; the other one looked like a punk--he had punk in his eyes, Jibril thought, so he'd have to chance that the kid would have stage fright. The kid with the box cutter yelled something at him that was drowned out by the conductor's announcement that the train was arriving in Times Square. "You lucky this is our stop," he heard the would be assailant say. "You lucky this is our stop, punk!" The punk-looking one said, as they left the train.

As bizarre as it looked to the frightened passengers, Jibril actually chuckled to himself as his would-be attackers withdrew. He was thinking about how much he'd come to love her after first hating that instrument. Shit, there was a time he would have gladly given it away.

When his mother first sent him to Hassan, he resented it greatly. He felt deeply embarrassed lugging the fake leather trumpet case to and fro between lessons, while his friends enjoyed a game of ball. Why shouldn't he be having fun? he thought. Why not? he concluded, so for a while he just pretended to go (she'd never know). "How was your lesson?" his mother would ask when she got home. And he'd always tell her it was great. In fact it was, he was having fun playing with his friends and his mother was happy he was taking lessons. It couldn't be better.

One day he came upstairs to get some lemonade before rushing back outside. His mom was opening the door just as he was going back out.

"Hey Chris," she said cheerfully, "come here I've got something for you."

"Aw man, we were gonna play basketball," he moaned.

"It'll just take a sec," she promised. "Come here, sit down, let me show you what I got for you. So how was today's lesson?" she asked, while taking off her coat.

"It was great!" he replied enthusiastically.

"Oh that's funny," she said, while taking off her shoes. That's really funny, because I spoke to Hassan today." Jibril felt his heart flutter as his mother kept smiling. "And he said that you didn't show up today."

" . . . but," he protested.

"In fact, he said that you haven't shown up all week," she said still smiling.

"But," was all he could muster.

"Butt is right Chris, because I need to beat your butt. What do you think this is? I'm spending my hard-earned money to pay for these lessons, and you're outside playing!" Her voice rose in anger. "What do you think this is?"

"But . . ."

"But nothing. What's wrong with you, boy?"

"But my friends."

"Your friends what?"

"My friends were making fun of me, carrying that trumpet case. It's like I have to go to school even after we get out of school, and they get to go play."

"Look," she said tenderly, "if they're making fun of you, they're really not your friends. Besides you shouldn't be so concerned about what people say."

"I don't care, why can't I just be like everybody else?"

"Because you're not like everybody else-- you're my son, you're special. Now look, I know that you may not like it, but believe me you're going to appreciate it one day."

"But . . ."

"But nothing. I don't want to hear it anymore. You're going to these lessons. You hear me boy?"

"Dag . . ."

"Don't 'dag' me boy. Now go to your room."

He picked up the trumpet case. He hated it. He was furious and was very tempted to toss it out of his window, but he knew his mother would kill him. The next morning he said that he felt too sick to go to school, but his mother was unsympathetic, and told him that he had to go anyway. "And don't forget your lesson this afternoon. I'll be expecting a call from Hassan when you get there."

"Damn," he thought.

He resented Hassan for a long time after that, and he would constantly neglect his trumpet pretending to forget that it needed cleaning. On top of that, he was struggling with the practice regimen, and it didn't seem to him like he was making any progress. He'd taken to sneaking the trumpet case around in a large shopping bag, not that it made a difference--the teasing didn't cease. He hated lugging that trumpet case around.

But not anymore, not after they'd spent so much time together and grown so close over the years. He remembered the first time he made her sing, it was like a miracle. Hassan said that it was the culmination of all his hard work, but Jibril didn't care. It seemed like a miracle to him; considering how hard it was when he first started, it had to be a miracle, he thought. Once he could make her sing, some of the shame and embarrassment fell from his shoulders; he didn't want to carry her around in a shopping bag anymore. Even if his boys didn't like it, he knew he was on to something. Still though, in the back of his mind, he longed for the recognition of the brothas from around the way. Just a little dap, maybe a tenth of what he would get if he played college ball, that's all, just that little bit.

David Lamb

Chapter Sixteen

"I want the same thing you want, the same thing we all want, peace in our communities. Safe streets so that people can walk home without fear and trepidation, so that our mothers and wives will feel safe shopping in their own communities. I want these guns off these streets so that we won't have to read about an innocent child being shot every other week. I want young brothers to look forward to a future at Harvard, Princeton, and Yale instead of Rikers, Comstock, and Ossining. We have the same goals. We may not agree on how to get there, but I deeply believe that we share the same goals."

Walking through the streets in his trademark tortoise shell glasses, silver-buttoned blue blazer, white cotton shirt, solid red power tie, khaki pants and black-tasseled loafers, he looked more like a young teacher than a would-be Congressman. An academic star since elementary school, Charlie Stokes had been tapped for leadership since he'd received a standing ovation at a fifth grade assembly for his passionate delivery of Martin Luther King's *'I Have A Dream'* speech, ever since he'd attended Andover through the "A Better Chance" program. He was determined to live up to his promise. He'd shone brilliantly as an economics student at Princeton, before returning to the City and graduating from Columbia's business and law schools simultaneously. While in law school, he'd volunteered at Assemblyman Al Vann's office, doing substantive legislative analysis and walking the streets

getting out the vote, learning to meet and greet and
greet and meet people. He was a born politician, an
eternal optimist who never ever spoke in defeatist
tones. Charlie Stokes radiated confidence and
ambition. He had a smile that brightened the greyest
sky. If you let him get on a roll, he would recite
chapter and verse the history of Black politics in New
York, particularly Bedford-Stuyvesant's politics.
He'd studied them all, from Bertram Barker's 1948
election to the City Council as both Brooklyn and
Bed-Stuy's first Black elected official through Shirley
Chisholm's election to Congress in 1968 up through
the most recent detailed intimate local clubhouse
politics. And in the back of his mind, his place in the
borough's political legacy was already written.

Hassan had been an early supporter of his,
even though some thought Charlie was too young to
run for Congress and hadn't paid his dues yet.

"We need to rethink our whole approach to
this drug problem," Charlie started politely (he was on
alien turf and knew that he had an uphill climb).
"Instead of looking at users as criminals who need to
be locked up, we need to see them as what they are,
sick people, sick people who need to be helped. We
need to start looking at this not just as a simple crime
issue. We need to start taking a public health
approach."

Hassan had invited Charlie to address the
Imam and the other members of the Mosque's board.
Even though he knew that Charlie's ideas about
legalization would be a sticking point, to say the least,

David Lamb

he still wanted him to get a hearing.

"With all due respect," Charlie began, "Bill Clinton has declared war on drugs, George Bush declared war on drugs, Ronald Reagan and Richard Nixon both declared war on drugs, yet the drug problem is worse now than it was under Nixon. Meanwhile, the government is diverting so many resources into fighting this 'war' that it's taking away from monies that could be used for schools, for libraries, for hospitals. So now because of this failed war we've got two problems, crime on the streets keeping businesses out and terrorizing innocent folks, and a whole generation tied to the justice system.

"It seems to me that if we haven't put a dent in drugs since Nixon declared war, that we might at least want to explore the possibility of alternative strategies. For example, just consider for one moment, just consider, if we took a public health approach, treating drug abuse as a medical problem rather than a criminal issue. It's possible that we might be able to make more progress."

"So, you want to legalize drugs," the Imam countered. "Son, in our religion it tells us to enjoin the good and forbid the wrong."

"Brother, please, hear me out. I'm not calling for legalization, not in the sense of drugs being sold over the counter like cigarettes and alcohol. I view it more as a policy of "medicalization," where drug abuse would be treated as a disease. Where the government--not drug dealers--would control price, distribution, and access."

The Trumpet Is Blown

"Some might say they already do," someone snickered.

David Lamb

Chapter Seventeen

"You no eat pork?" the man behind the plexiglass asked.

"Nah, man," Jibril said with a laugh at his recognition that just moments before he hadn't believed Bilal when he'd told him that he'd discovered a No-Pork Chinese restaurant along Fourth Avenue near Atlantic. He couldn't believe he hadn't even known that the restaurant existed. "Nah, I don't eat pork," he answered, laughing at himself. Even as they were getting off the train, he thought that Bilal would stop and say that he was only playing. As they approached the store, though, he saw the words "NO-PORK" in big red letters over a bright yellow background. He had to laugh. It looked like any other Chinese restaurant in the 'hood, but right at the top of the menu in large bold letters it said "NO-PORK". The only detraction was that they could have spent more money on the decor. The mauve-colored floor tiles needed replacing, and there was no place to sit down--it was strictly take out. It had been so so long since he'd had Chinese food, though. He took a healthy whiff and let the exotic aromas sink in and entice him. Behind the plexiglass protector he saw the chef busily working magic on a giant wok. He looked longingly at the day's specials taped to the front of the plexiglass: boneless chicken-breast with fried rice; boneless beef rib tips; fried beef won ton and General Tso's chicken with fried rice.

"Can I get a chicken fried rice, please?" he

The Trumpet Is Blown

asked, sticking to what was most familiar.

"No problem."

David Lamb

Chapter Eighteen

"Let me get a chicken fried rice."

The Trumpet Is Blown

Chapter Nineteen

"Let me get a chicken fried rice."

Chapter Twenty

"Let me get a chicken fried rice."

The Trumpet Is Blown

Chapter Twenty-one

"Let me . . ."

". . . get a chicken fried rice," Jimmy Chin said, with a laugh. Jibril had to laugh too. He'd been coming to the 'No-Pork Chinese Restaurant' so much that Jimmy could finish his sentences.

"Yo' Jibril, dag, how much you be comin' here?!" Bilal asked.

"Yo', Bilal, I think I need help, man, I'm addicted to this place."

"Yeah, you might be. I've heard of this condition before, man, you better get it checked out," he said, through a chuckle.

As Jimmy started to hand Jibril his order he paused, and then looked at Jibril in a way that one could tell the wheels were turning. "Jibril, how's your trumpet playing?" Jimmy asked.

"It's going well."

"Good, I've got a deal for you." Jibril was puzzled and furrowed his brow inquisitively.

"I want you and your band to play at my son's wedding."

"Well I . . ."

"No, I want you, okay?"

"Well . . ."

"I'll pay you $500."

"I'll do it!" Jibril said with a big grin, as he thought about how this was a down payment on the studio money he'd been hoping for.

"Good. Here, I want you and your friend try

107

this Chinese ginseng tea. I made a special brew for my son, so that I will have many grandchildren."

"But I thought Korean ginseng was the best," a smirking Jibril said.

"You see a billion Koreans or a billion Chinese?" Jimmy shot back through a light chuckle.

"Oh," Jibril said conceding the point.

As they left the restaurant, Jibril could hardly contain his happiness at the thought of his luck. Meanwhile, Bilal was nearly doubled over in laughter, and with his eyes tearing he finally toppled over in uncontrollable hysterics.

"Wha . . . What's so funny?" Jibril managed between burst of laughter.

"You!" Bilal managed to squeeze out.

"Me?"

"Yes, you!"

"Why me?"

"'Cause, 'cause man, what you know about playin' at a Chinese wedding, what kinda music you gonna play?"

"Oh . . ." Jibril paused. He hadn't thought of that, he'd just heard $500, and everything else went blank.

The Trumpet Is Blown

Chapter Twenty-two

Walking home as night pummeled day into submission, Jibril munched the last corner of the mini bean pie he had left over from lunch. As he approached his building, he thought that he recognized the cheery figure holding court in front chatting up a regal storm. The voice had a familiar ring. "But it couldn't be him," he said to himself. So many brothas he knew went in and out of jail so often that it was hard to keep track--who went in, when they went in, what they went in for, and when they were expected back on the block. As he got closer, he was sure that it really was him though.

"Yo', what up Pound?" Jibril greeted him cheerfully.

"Nuttin' man, it's your world, Ah'm jus' a squirrel tryin' to get a nut," Pound responded cheerfully, while extending his hand to slap Jibril's. Pound was the most cheerful recidivist Jibril had ever known. In fact, Jibril could never figure out what Pound was going in and out of the system for. To look at him belied his essential recidivist nature. He was always laughing and joking. True, he didn't seem to have much (if any) ambition, but Jibril could never associate him with any actual criminal activity. He'd just be here one week, gone the next.

"How you doing, man, talk to me, wussup, you gonna be home for good, or what?" Jibril asked, his voice rising with hope and encouragement.

"Most definitely, man, I ain't got no intention

on going back," he said cheerfully, while extending his hand to slap Jibril's. *"Youknowwhatah'msayin'*," he said cheerfully while extending his hand to slap Jibril's. "I took me some college courses while I was up in that hole, and Ah'm about to get down wit' this program at Brooklyn College," he said cheerfully, while extending his hand to slap Jibril's.

Jibril was always amazed at how good brothas look when they first get home. Pound's forty ounce gut was gone, his hair was freshly cut, and he was talking the right talk. Jibril hoped that *this* time, he could stick it out.

"That's peace, man, that's great, I'm glad to hear you're makin' that move."

"Got's to," he said cheerfully, while extending his hand to slap Jibril's.

"But I see one thing hasn't changed."

"What?"

"You're still a damn serial habitual hand shaker," a laughing Jibril said. Pound got his nickname from his perpetual seeking of, well, a pound. Every second or third sentence you could count on Pound either extending his hand to slap you five, or putting his hand out--waiting for you to slap him five. It got to the point where if a crew of brothas were engaging him in a conversation, they would rotate who stood closest to him, otherwise he'd wear your hand out! Today he was in rare form. He'd just gotten un-incarcerated a few days earlier, and he was so happy to be out and so excited about his future plans that he was slapping five at the end of every sentence!

As Jibril bid adieu to Pound and walked toward his building he could sense by the way everyone was looking at him that something was terribly wrong, but he had no idea what it could be, until Bilal ran up to him and said, "Don't worry, she's all right!"

"All right? She who?"

"Your mom's . . ."

"What?!" He could feel the blood rushing.

"Yeah, this pookie snatched her purse, but don't worry, he gonna get got, believe that."

"Yo' I gotta go see my mom's," he said anxiously, while brushing past Bilal.

"Yo' I'll go wit' you . . ."

As he charged up the steps, Jibril's mind raced with thoughts of retaliation. He knew he had to step to the kid, or his mother would be a project target from that point on. He stormed into the house anxious to make sure that she was all right. He was surprised to find her sitting calmly at the kitchen table, slowly sipping a hot cup of peppermint tea. She looked up at her son and gave him a faint, reassuring smile. "I'm okay," she said before he could ask.

"What happened? Who was it? Where did it . . . When did it happen?" He was so angry he wasn't giving her a chance to answer. "Are you okay?" He asked tenderly.

"I already told you I'm okay," she smiled, tapping his forehead with her small hand as he leaned over her. "The police were already here."

"So, what happened?"

"I don't want to talk about it right now. I'm going to lay down, I've got to go to work in the morning."

"But . . ."

All he got was a wave of the hand as she walked down the hall sipping her tea.

He hadn't called Shaun in a long time, but he needed a gun, and he knew Shaun would be able to set him up quickly. Unfortunately, or fortunately, he didn't get the cooperation he expected.

"Yo', yo' Jibril calm down, man, I don't think you wanna do that, man. You got shit going for you, don't fuck that up over some dumb shit, man," Shaun implored. He hated the thought that the one brotha he knew who was doing something on the positive tip was about to get caught up.

"Yo', man, fuck that I . . .," Jibril's anger was getting the best of him, he didn't want to hear it.

"Jibril! Jibril! What do you think you're doing?!" his mother demanded as she hung up his call. She'd been listening from the bathroom unbeknownst to Jibril, and she wasn't going to have her only son getting shot or shooting somebody over foolishness.

"I was just talkin' to my man . . ."

"Don't lie to me boy, I heard you."

"But . . ."

"But nothing boy, I didn't raise you to go chasing people in the street with guns."

"I wasn't . . ."

The Trumpet Is Blown

"What did I say, boy? Look Jibril," she paused, her voice suddenly turning tender, "I know you love your mother, but son, we're going to have to let the police handle this one."

"The police?! They. . ."

"They what? This is what they get paid to do. Right?! Right?!"

"Right," he said reluctantly, with little enthusiasm.

"Look, just take a shower and calm down. Okay? Will you do that for your mother?"

"Okay." He knew she was going to be watching him like a hawk this night, so he thought it best to pretend to go along.

She'd been watching him like a hawk for as long as he could remember. When he was a little boy, he would sometimes be annoyed with her, feeling that she was smothering him. As he got older, however, he came to appreciate having a mom like his mom. When he was younger, all of his friends wished that she was their mother. He remembered when he was in the fourth grade, and she decided to go back to school--to college. He would come upstairs dirty from the day's activities, and she would order him directly to a bath, while she tried to figure out "this new math," as she put it. Despite the difficulties, she persevered and finished, graduating with a bachelor's degree in accounting from Long Island University's downtown Brooklyn campus. She was able to attend college at night through a program her job sponsored. Jibril was

David Lamb

proud of her. He remembered her arguing with his teachers if they manifested even the slightest, most minute possibility that their own prejudice would preclude her son's appointment with greatness. He appreciated her more than he could ever express in words. He saw, he knew what happened without a loving, strong, supportive mother.

She knew he knew she was going to be hawking him that night, and that he was just pretending to go along, but she thought it best to pretend that he had fooled her, and prayed that he would actually calm down. She was going to be keeping watch though. When Jibril got in the shower, she called Hassan and asked him to talk some sense into her son. When he got out of the shower, and his mother told him that Nsinga had called, he figured she'd called Hassan, but he went along and called Nsinga anyway.

That night he passionately caressed her in his hands, his eyes marveling at her beauty, stunned by the grandeur of the initialed birth stones he'd bought for her, his fingertips lovingly surveying her every compartment, then he gently laid her on his bed and began undressing her, exploring her inner workings. It had been a month since they'd been so intimate-- now, he lovingly bathed her with lukewarm water, then tenderly dried her with his towel. Then he began oiling her in all the appropriate places--her valves needed frequent oiling. Then he began lightly lubricating her tuning slides with mineral oil (she needed lubricating once a month in order not to become too tight and stiff). After making sure that the slides and valves were properly treated, he had to be sure to put the proper valves in the appropriate chambers; if not, she wouldn't function properly. He needed her, needed her to work properly, needed her centering, calming effect.

He was trying to keep his head above water in a world drowning in confusion, where senseless death abounded. His mother had been attacked, crackheads on his back. He needed demo money. It seemed as though it was all coming down on him just as he was trying to stay focused on the fast approaching Jazz Ahead deadline. He was anxious and needed her to reassure him. Embracing each other, that night they serenaded the projects from a glowing gravel-strewn rooftop lit by the light of a lone star framed by the luminous cast of a bright, crescent-shaped moon. The notes, carried by a gentle night breeze magically, momentarily soothing the savage beasts below, and drowning out, for one mystical moment, the deadly symphonic sound of syncopated gunfire.

The beautiful lyricism was hypnotic. Fiend was the first to fall under its enchanting spell. He was just about to light his pipe when the first notes reached his ears. He was frozen as the cascading sound waves penetrated his fog-strewn consciousness and without even realizing it the pipe tumbled from his hand.

Shaun was in the midst of a transaction when he was transfixed by the horn's eerie wail. It seemed as though all heads turned toward the

David Lamb

heavens, literally desiring to see the sounds.

Suddenly thunder echoed in the distance providing a bass-like undercurrent. The clouds opened, and the light pitter-patter of rain dropped like shimmering cymbals. As he blew through his pain, the soaring notes rose to a furious crescendo as lightning crackled, brightening the night sky.

The Trumpet Is Blown

Chapter Twenty-three

In a state of frightened despair, fleeing rumors of an eminent beat down, with nowhere else to go, Marcus checked himself into a seven-day rehabilitation program--not looking for true rehabilitation, just looking for a place to stay and a chance to get a temporary escape from his crack creditors. While he was there, a Narcotics Anonymous outreach meeting was taking place, and as a part of the program, he was forced to attend. He was reluctant, angry, and in denial. That was for "those people," he thought. He wasn't addicted. He just liked taking a little hit every now and then. Those people didn't have anything to tell him.

Despite his lack of interest, the program required that he attend two meetings a week. He sat in the back of the room with his arms folded in defiant indifference. A well-dressed, very sophisticated older Black woman got up to speak.

"What's she doin' here?" Marcus asked himself, not realizing that you couldn't always judge a book by its cover.

"At first I started out just using a little cocaine on the weekend," Charlene began. "Friday, Saturday, but never on Sunday, because I had to calm down for work. I was making good money then, and I had been convinced that cocaine was the bourgie drug, for those of us rising up the social ladder, the buppie socializing drug, and that's how I thought of it--just something for a little weekend fun. I didn't realize that the cocaine was slowly taking control of my will. I didn't even see it coming. One day I met my girlfriends for lunch, and I saw them each take a little hit. I was a little surprised; after all, we had to return to work that day. 'What were they doing?' I wondered. They told me I was being square, that I was making a mountain out of a molehill. It was just like coffee, they said, just a little picker-upper to get through a long day, so I bought into it, wanting to be hip, and took a hit. Before I knew what was what, what used to be a weekend thing was soon an everyday thing. I found myself sneaking little hits to make it through the day. After a while, I wasn't eating lunch anymore, no, lunch time was a chance for me to sneak away and get a one on one. And at first, at first, it seemed cool. Work that used to take me all afternoon to finish, I was doing in half the time. I felt like a superwoman, nothing could stop me. But the problem was I started needing more and more coke to get back to that initial high, and every time I would come down, I would feel lower than I felt the last time I came down! My habit, even though I hadn't realized it was a habit yet, had started getting worse, and I needed to feed it. My work started to suffer as my lunch hour got longer, I started feeling weak from not eating, and coming in late or not coming in at all. I became a liability. I even got caught sneaking in my co-workers' desks stealing here and there. No one could understand it, since I'd been such a good worker. Soon I found myself unemployed. I still had a good resume and at first I was able to get some decent temp bookkeeping work and I was able to keep my habit and my apartment, so I wasn't realizing how fast things were falling apart. Soon enough, my habit was spiraling out of control, getting worse and worse, and I started losing my temp jobs. Still, I figured I could handle it. I was wrong. I was three months behind on my rent, but I still wouldn't quit, I had started caring more about the cocaine than my job, my family. I started conning money from my mother . . . Thank God, as I understand him, for my brotha forcing me to come to an N.A. meeting with him. I didn't even know that he had had a problem, he'd kept it undercover, but he could tell from his own experiences what was happening to me without me even telling him. I tried to deny it at first, but he kept after me, told me that N.A. had helped him wrestle with his problem. I've been clean for eight years now, but it's still one day at a time."

"Thank you Charlene," Leon, the short, rotund brotha who'd introduced himself as the secretary said, before asking if there was anyone in the audience who'd like to testify. When they started, it sruck Marcus as bizarre, admitting your addiction--bizarre.

"Hi, my name is Aaron, I'm an addict, and I have thirteen days in."

"Hi Aaron, welcome," the crowd greeted him back, warmly and supportively.

"Hi, my name is Abdul-Rahim, and I'm an addict, and I have thirteen years in."

"Hi Abdul-Rahim, welcome," again he was greeted with a warm, supportive applause. Then a sister stood up, haggard-looking and severely undernourished; yet, when Marcus looked deeper he saw in her warm brown eyes a profound look of resolve.

"Hi, my name is Luisa and Ah'm an addict, this is my first day, and, and," at first she was fighting back the tears, then, suddenly, she was wiping them away as they cascaded down her cheeks. "And, my grandmother just died in Puerto Rico, and I'm so fuck'd up on this crack, I couldn't even go to her funeral. I just pray that ya'll support me, 'cause, 'cause, this crack, this crack, is kickin' my ass ya'll, 'scuse me, but I, I need help ya'll."

"Hi Luisa, welcome," the crowd assured her, several people rushing over and giving her supportive hugs. Then Charlene spoke directly to Luisa and told her that just because she'd been clean for eight years, that Luisa shouldn't look at her and say wow, because no matter how long you've been away--it's still one day at a time, whether you've been clean fifteen years or fifteen days, it's just one day at a time. Then she asked if there were any other newcomers who would like to declare themselves, while glancing at Marcus.

Marcus saw himself leap to his feet and declare, "Hi my name is Marcus, and I'm an addict." But he was still sitting. "Why am I still sitting?" he asked himself. "Because you're not an addict," he told himself. "Shee-it, I'm not gettin' up in front of all these people and sayin' I'm no addict. I ain't no addict, I just got a little problem, shee-it, it ain't really a problem, I can stop." He was at war with himself,

humility doing battle with pride, shame and despair--
and humility was losing. "Man, fuck this I ain't stayin'
here, this is wack." Marcus got up in a fit of anger,
knocking over his chair, as he stormed out.

"Don't leave before the miracle happens,"
Charlene implored.

"It gets greater later," a seated brotha shouted
out to him, but their words fell on deaf ears. Marcus
didn't want to hear them, didn't want to acknowledge
his problem, and because he didn't, he was doomed.

David Lamb

Chapter Twenty-four

"Yo', word creeped back who it was that snatched your mom's pocket book," Pound said in a low, deadly, serious tone.

"Word? Who the fuck was it?" Jibril asked his blood boiling with fury.

"Yo' it . . . Oh, shit, yo', what the . . . there he is right there, that nigga Fiend," but by the time he looked, all Jibril saw was a dirt blur whiz down the block. "Yo' Sharrief, grab him," he yelled, but it was too late. Fiend was off and running--the chase was on.

Racing through the streets like a scared sewer rat, Fiend was as petrified as Ian Smith on Judgement Day. He knew he'd pay for snatching Ms. Thomas' pocketbook right in the neighborhood, but he couldn't help it, the crack had been seductively calling his name, and he'd never been able to resist her. As he flew through the night, the sweat pelted his face like Uzi spray, his heart kicked his chest, and the raking pain in his side convinced him that he was having an appendicitis attack. Fiend's thoughts shot back to his youth when he was swift of foot. He tried to recall those smooth catlike moves he used to make playing touch football, but that was a thing of the past. His crack-racked, worn, and withered body could no longer respond with such precision. He was sorry now--sorry he had been stupid enough to snatch a pocketbook around the way. Soon he would be crying 'The Criminal Blues'. "I'm sorry, sorry-I-got-caught." He could hear the deadly stampede closing in on him, but there was light at the end of the tunnel. If he could just make it around the corner, he could cut through the alley and be off. "Ow! My fuckin' ankle!" He could hear the angry posse behind him in the distance. Too close for comfort. "These fucked up sidewalks," he screamed, still unable to see that the self-inflicted destruction was catching up to him. With mad desperation he pressed on, but his dirt-ladened clothes weighed him down like chain gang anklets, and the harder he ran, the heavier they got, and the more precious energy he recklessly expended clutching his once clean Kangol to his balding head. His skinny arms pumped frantically through the cool night air. As he glanced back in fright for a second, a fateful second, a frail tree branch reached out and snatched the Kangol from his head. He cried out as though mortally wounded. Every bone in his body wanted to turn back, but he dared not. As he ran, he grieved for the lost hat like a child who had just lost a beloved pet. To his utter dismay, Sharrief, a big bruising brotha who was rumored to be going to Iowa to play football, had burst to the front of the pursuing crowd. The pounding sound of Sharrief's feet fast approaching sounded to Fiend like Mike Tyson's bombs thudding against a haplessly prone Marvis Frazier. Suddenly Sharrief's hand darted out--stretching in desperation to reach Fiend, falling short of grabbing his shoulder, he managed to grabbed Fiend's left sneaker as the untied Nike came off in his massive right hand. With everything he had left Fiend vaulted pitifully in a desperate attempt to hop the gate that blocked his way at the end of the dead end alley. Unfortunately for Fiend he didn't have enough left. Crashing back to earth with a loud, painful thud onto the piss-stained, broken glass-filled street, his lower lip rapidly swelling and busted from the fall, Fiend was a pitiful sight, desperate and frightened. Sharrief barked angrily at him to get up, but he didn't have the strength to, and even if he did--he didn't have the courage. Sharrief gave him a swift, hard kick to encourage him. By the time Jibril caught up to them, he was in a rage and was about to imprint his Timberlands into Fiend's fear-emblazoned grill, when the radiant moonlight revealed Fiend's sweaty face, strikingly similar to Marcus' in his last days. Jibril was paralyzed by the resemblance. He slowly pulled his foot back from Fiend, who was by this time shamelessly begging for mercy, solemnly, but falsely, promising to pay back the stolen money. Jibril, stunned by the resemblance, was suddenly filled by the hope that he could do for Fiend what he couldn't do for his brother.   Carefully, as if approaching his prey, he bent down and spoke in slow, serious tones, smacking him on the head, hard, before catching himself, then smacking him upside the head again. Jibril was so angry that he could barely get the words out.

"Now, listen, muthafucka, the only reason your punk ass is gonna get outta here tonight is because I owe my brother one, and so I'm not going to beat your ass," he paused, looking away to calm himself, then looking back. "Too bad," he said with a joyously vengeful grin, "but you're gonna have to straighten your punk ass out, you're gonna have to make a change, man, you can't be livin' like this, not around here, not no more, you got to change this shit, man. Our mothers can't go to the store for fear of dealers shooting 'em or of someone like you snatchin' their purse. Fuck that! Now listen, this is what I want your punk ass to do--you gonna have to stop smoking that crack shit, or else every, and I mean every time I see you, Ah'm fuckin' you up, straight up. Now that might be cold but it be's that way sometimes. Now get the fuck out my face."

"Yo', you just gonna let him go?" Sharrief bellowed disapprovingly between deep breaths.

"Man, it's not even worth it."

"Nah, man, fuck that, not after I ran all this way, he got to pay something. Yo'! Yo' man, I'm talkin' to you," Sharrief roared at the frightened Fiend. "Yo', check this out, right," said Sharrief, sounding like the voice of reason, "either I'm beating that ass, or you givin' up the sneakers, it's your choice." Fiend didn't waste any time, in a second, his remaining sneaker was slipped off. Sharrief grabbed it with a brown paper bag that had been covering an empty Ol' E bottle. As Sharrief walked away he kicked Fiend, and told him to disappear before he got really mad. Needless to say, Fiend vanished.

He'd been vanishing for a while now--disappearing, withdrawing further into his addiction. Wounded, he stumbled--searching for a dark corner to crawl into, to retreat, to vanish. Intermittently, he

David Lamb

peeked wearily at the night sky imagining the stars peering down at him accusatorialy.

With only those accusatory stars as witnesses, Fiend chuckled as a family gathered to renew old acquaintances.

"Yo' C, you lookin' kinda fuck'd up. What's up wit' that, man? You needs to put on some shoes." Gazing up through blurred vision from the open fire hydrant where he was kneeling trying to use the dripping water to clean his fresh wounds, Fiend saw a familiar figure slowly begin to take form.

"What's up little brother? How you like me now?!" he said, in a bad, sad impersonation of Kool Moe Dee.

"I don't, you all fuck'd up."

"C'mon little brother, Ah'm the one who put you down in the game," Fiend said, trying to gloriously recall his past.

"Yeah, but you fell off. I told you about that masterin' your high bullshit. The only way to master this shit is not to use."

"Yeah," he paused thoughtfully, "I should've listened," Fiend said bowing and shaking his head in momentary humiliation. "Yo' listen, little bro, you think you could hook me up?" he blurted out, suddenly full of hope.

Looking around to make sure that the stars were still the only witnesses, Benjamin Franklin gave his older brother two Jumbos.

"Clean your shit up!" He said emphatically,

126

before rushing away to make sure he hadn't been seen. "Clean your shit up and I might put you down," he said, as he walked away.

Later that evening in a familiar Ol' E ritual, the earlier hunt was celebrated around a garbage can fire which had been set to dispose of Fiend's sneakers. Sharrief began the ceremony by pouring a miniscule amount of beer on the curb, then taking a gracious swig from the bottle. "We are gathered here today to pay tribute to a raggedy pair of huhnid dollar sneakers," he chanted, in his best imitation of a Richard Pryor impersonation of a charlatan black preacher. "Fifty-dollar sneakers, ain't got no job, tell me how you do it when times are hard," the crowd spontaneously sang in unison. Sharrief continued, "The owner, or should I say the previous wearer of these sneakers, 'cause he probably stole them from someone, is a filthy individual, the swine of the earth, can I get an amen?"

"Amen," the crowd bellowed with laughter.

"Now I know we're angry that we weren't able to apply some serious physical punishment to this individual this evening, but let us take this shoe, his shoe, and cast it into the flames only symbolizing what a foul brotha eventually has comin' to him."

And with that humorous, yet solemn, tribute, the Nikes were deposited into the flames.

"Yo', Jibril, take a swig," Sharrief urged.

"Nah, Ah'm cool."

"Yo', how come you don't get stimulated?"

Sharrief asked.

"C'mon now, you know I ain't down wit' no intoxicants, my brotha. But, yo', check this out, even if I was, alcohol is a depressant, so how am I going to get stimulated off that, and second of all about a million brothas done drank out that bottle already. But can I ask you a question my brotha?"

"Indeed."

"If Old English is the power, how come black folk so poor?"

"'If Old English is the power how come black folk so poor?' Damn, that's a good question." Sharrief admitted as he drank deep from the well.

"Yo' Jibril, remember when you first started playin'?" Sharrief asked, while taking another healthy swig, feeling a slight buzz from the brew. "That shit was funny, your little ass carrying that big case--we used to get all over you. And then, and then," he said laughing, "and then you tried to hide that shit wit' that big shoppin' bag. And Bilal busted you. And we all started callin' you 'Shoppin' Bag'." He was howling at this point. "Shoppin' Bag!" he screamed. Everyone was howling now.

Jibril's face tightened in anger even though a part of him wanted to laugh too. He had to admit it was funny. "Shoppin' Bag," that name haunted his early adolescence and was why they had never actually heard him play. "Remember that?" Sharrief asked, still laughing.

"Yeah, I remember that, [nigga]," he thought. "That shit wasn't all that damn funny," he said, even though he couldn't help but laugh himself.

"Aw c'mon, lighten up, nigga, chill," Sharrief's words were stretching out now, the alcohol buzz had him feeling ripe. "Yo', bust it, chill, let me talk, let me talk, I'm tryin' to be serious."

"What nigga . . .," Jibril laughed at Sharrief's slight swagger, "you tryin' to be serious? Didn't you just tell me to lighten up?" he laughed.

"Aw-ight, aw-ight, nigga chill."

"What? Spill . . . it . . . out."

"I just wanted to say . . . I just wanted to say . . ." He was almost choked up.

"What nigga?" Jibril couldn't keep from chuckling as Sharrief's eyes became increasingly serious.

"I just wanted to say, I'd never really heard you play before, but," he took a small swig, wiping the spillover with his left forearm, "but, the other night," he took another swig, "the other night, that shit you played . . . that shit fucked me all the way up!" Jibril smiled. "I mean that was the most beautiful shit I ever heard."

"Word, it was like that shit was all around us!" Pound said.

"Yeah, yeah, it was like that shit was all around us," Sharrief agreed. "It made us feel real good."

"Damn," Jibril said. He'd never felt prouder.

"I jus' wanted to say, keep it up, man, we all proud of you." Putting the 40 in his left hand Sharrief raised his mighty right hand and slapped Jibril a hearty five, pulling him into him as they hugged with genuine affection.

"Thanks man, you'll never know how much that means to me," Jibril said with sincerity and seriousness.

"Ay, yo' Jibril, ain't that Landa over there gettin' high wit' her homegirls?" Bilal inquired.

"I guess it is."

"So, what's up wit' that?"

"Yo', that's on her. Ah'm not her father, you know, I just gotta be me, and if she can't accept that, fuck it," he said with more than a hint of anger and machismo, as though he'd taken his stand and was through with her, with no part of his heart and soul phased whatsoever.

"Man, you know them kids they wit' just wanna turn her out."

"What can I do? Ah'm not going to be chasing behind her." While Jibril felt that he was right, he could not understand why any sista would rather be with a drug dealer. And as much as he hated to admit it, he was uncomfortable because he was still attracted to her. In part he was ashamed (he could hear Nsinga's words ringing in his ears) because it really bordered on pure physical attraction. She wasn't the most knowledgeable sista in the world, her lips had puffed far too many Phillies and she drank entirely too much cheap liquor. Still, she was beautiful. Her ebony skin glowed in the moonlight, her pink lips gorgeously contrasted with her dark complexion, and she had long, shapely arms and legs. Jibril was just enthralled. Whenever he saw her he felt the pull.

"Yo', Ah'm out. I've got to get up early tomorrow. Good lookin' out; I owe all ya'll. All right? Peace," he said, as he walked away, sneaking a peak at Landa out the corner of his right eye.

Back in the days when Jibril was still Chris, after a long fruitless summer of chasing Landa, Chris had somehow managed to cajole her into coming over his house late one Sunday night. It was three days before the start of the ninth grade. Chris' grandmom was in the back sleeping like a hibernating bear--just call her Yogi. His mom had gone to visit his aunt. Having finally finessed Landa into coming over, Chris was bubbling with anticipation. "Ring!" went the buzz of the doorbell.

He got up slowly from the kitchen chair where he had been waiting like a tense cat trapped in a corner, claws at the ready. As he walked to the door, he struggled to keep the smile off his face, but he couldn't help it. No matter how hard he tried, he had a "Kool Aid" smile. As he reached the door, his hand trembled as he turned the lock and gently pulled the door open, "Shaun, what are you doing here?"

"Me, T, and Sleepy are gettin' ready to play spades, we want to know if you want to play partners."

"Nah man, I got this girl comin' over."

"Get outta here!"

"Word em up."

"Let me hide behind the chair?"

"Come on, dude."

"Nah, Ah'm just playin', I'll catch you later."

Finally he left. Chris started back to the kitchen, exasperated, thinking that because it was drizzling outside Landa might use the rain as an excuse not to show up. Suddenly, the doorbell rang again. Chris got his 'cool' together and strolled to the door. Aaahh, there was Landa, shining like a Fon princess! It was hard for Chris to believe, but he couldn't help but notice that she was a little nervous too, and he allowed himself an internal smile over that fact. He invited her in. He just knew she was going to sit on the couch, but instead she sat in the lounge chair, temporarily foiling his plans. Luck was on his side, however, because when he turned on the radio it was just in time to catch <u>Tender Lover</u> by the Force M.D.s, and of course he had to weave it into his rap. Unfortunately, he sang like a frog with the mumps, but to his utter amazement, she was going for it. Eventually he talked her into sitting next to him on the couch. As he put his unsteady arm around her shoulder, Chris couldn't believe this was actually happening. He felt as though he were outside of his body, watching what was happening--a viewer, as opposed to a participant. As the gap between their lips slowly closed, Chris expected to wake up disappointed that he was only dreaming. To his surprise he wasn't, and moments later they were soul mates, embracing with that gentle first embrace shiver. The windows were closed, and the steam from their

The Trumpet Is Blown

heat fogged them.

Chris was so happy, and moving so fast that Landa asked why his mind was one track, he said because he 'preferred the Concord to the Amtrak,' asked her to make like a flapjack, flip on her back and sizzle, requested that she listen to the drizzle, please be his pumpkin, and help him unbutton, but just as he was ready to pull the rabbit out the hat, he heard a squeak and a creak--the door cracked, what can one say, it was wic wic wack, his moms was back, he was played, and it was like that.

David Lamb

Chapter Twenty-five

"Nsinga, you're so pretty, why don't you ever, you know, show yourself off? You would have so many guys sweatin' you!" Carla cajoled in her familiar singsong fashion.

"I don't want so many guys sweatin' me."

"You still stuck on Jibril?"

Nsinga blushed before responding. "It's not about him, it's about me. If a guy is going to like me I want him to like me for me. For my mind, my personality, my character, not 'cause I got a phat butt."

"So you're sayin' that you don't want guys to think you're pretty?" Carla asked with a hint of skepticism.

"Well c'mon, we all want to be pretty. I am sayin', though, that it's more to it than that. A lot more, and that I don't want it to be just, or even mostly, a physical thing. I mean, how is that going to work?"

"See girl, you just got your head all confused by that Africa and Islam stuff. I'm sorry, but to me, them muzlem guys is just too damn strict like they wanna rule you. I can't get wit' that."

"Well, Carla, like I told you before, Islam's not the problem, the problem is men. Some men want to act like, for women, Islam means submission to men, but it doesn't; for men and women it means submission to God. That's why I always say that you've got to distinguish between *'Hislam'* and Islam.

The Trumpet Is Blown

I mean when you look at Prophet Muhammad's first wife, Khadija."

"Like your moms?"

"Right, like my moms. Khadija was forty years old when she and Prophet Muhammad got married. She had her own business. He worked for her. And she was the one who proposed to him. She was in control of her own life."

"You know them muzlem girls," Benjamin said, while squinting his eyes and sucking his teeth knowingly, as Nsinga and Carla walked past on their way to the train station. "They be tryin' to look all refined, but you know they be gettin' busy wit' the closed door behind. All you gotta do is have tight game, and you know my game is tight," Benjamin said with much self assurance, before punctuating his point with a high five to Glock, who couldn't resist adding his own twist.

"Word, I heard they be putting the mojo on a nigga in bed," Glock said.

"Damn," Benjamin exclaimed, "I don't care if she muzlem, Jehovah's Witness or mufuckin' Greek Orthodox, a nigga like me got game for that ass! Like Landa, I haven't hit that yet, but you know me, Ah'm a have her like Priest had his women--all over the tip and deep in check!"

"And besides, you know Jibril's got a problem." Nsinga said, going back to Carla's prior question. A tantalizing pause further wetting Carla's already thirsty curiosity.

"What?!" Carla asked anxiously.

135

David Lamb

"Well," Nsinga whispered anxiously, looking around as if to make sure no one was listening. "Well," she repeated, "you can't say anything."

"I won't," Carla promised.

"You promise."

"Yes," she promised again.

"He's a man," Nsinga responded through a chuckle.

"Yeah, can't trust 'em," Carla agreed, while slapping Nsinga a high five of her own.

"Now, you're catching on." She sang approvingly. "Can we go now, so I can get started braiding your hair, please? I'm not trying to do a salon marathon, okay?"

Nsinga loved braiding hair. For her it was an extension of her sculpting, of her art. Over the years she'd studied and collected pictures of dozens of African braided hairstyles from the simple to the intricate, the austere to the astonishing. All of her friends loved for her to braid their hair, too. They loved the relaxing, soothing calm of her magical hands tenderly oiling their scalps. She loved making straight lines; sometimes she would part the hair in and out and around itself creating wonderfully stunning styles, quietly reminiscent of Hausa or Zulu wall painting patterns. There was something communal about her approach; the air would be filled with the spirit of sisterhood. This was 'women's time'--time alone to converse and communicate without the sometimes obtrusive presence of men. Sounds of her favorite African singers from Aster Aweke to Miriam Makeba would fill the room and they'd be magically transported to an African village, as images and memories of little girls jumping rope would flood the forefront of Nsinga's thoughts. The atmosphere inspiring her creative and dexterous hands to skillfully weave in double-dutch fashion, interlocking the strands of hair into beautiful works of art. As unorthodox as it seemed, she'd actually included pictures of some of her best works in her portfolio as part of her college applications. Her top choice was Cooper Union in the Village, because it was in New York, and because her favorite artist, Elizabeth Catlett, had gone there.

David Lamb

Chapter Twenty-six

As Jibril approached the front door, the unmistakable smell of chitlings singed his nostrils, and he felt his stomach do a somersault as he reeled and staggered under the assault of the wretched smell. "Damn," he said to himself, "everything but the "oink" must be getting cooked in that joint, but it ain't no point in harassing her grandmother, 'cause if she's like mine she's definitely a swine lover, pig-feet grubber, cooking in a tub of lard, bacon, ham, grits, and Spam. I mean damn, can I get a helping hand?"

Jibril braced himself as he knocked on the door, because he knew he had to act normal so that he wouldn't offend Landa's grandmother. He paused before knocking, wavering in indecision. Should he turn on his heels, or plunge ahead? Too late. Landa opened the door slowly, smiling brightly. It had been at least two years since Jibril had come to her house, and she was glad to see him. She wore a fuchsia-colored cotton shirt that stopped just above her bejeweled belly button. Her curvaceous hips dove sharply into her loose-fitting black jeans, and sky-blue anklet socks highlighted her slender ebony ankles. Jibril felt a hot flash, and made his way into the living room and sat on the couch. On the wall in the hallway he spied a beautifully-framed picture of a white Jesus, blue eyes and long stringy blond hair. Landa sat in the chair across from him, admiring his razor sharp fade. Before they could say anything, Landa's grandmother's shadow haunted the living room entrance.

"Well, Landa, aren't you going to introduce me to your friend?"

"Oh, Jibril, this is my grandma. Grandma, this is Jibril."

"Nice to meet you Mrs. Root." His smile was so wide that his jaws ached.

"Nice to meet you, young man. Listen, I've got some chitlings in the kitchen if you're hungry." And just like that, Jibril's best laid plans were on the verge of being torn asunder. Seconds seemed like hours as Jibril's mind combed the recesses of his brain searching for the perfect response. Landa's stomach fizzled, and her eyes glazed over. Jibril did not want to say that he didn't eat pork, lest her grandmom start barking up his tree, but he didn't want to be a hypocrite either. After not so carefully weighing his options, he decided to avoid any head on collision and rather to try to avoid any conflict.

"No thanks Mrs. Root, I just ate." Landa's grandmother had her man on the ropes now, and she knew it, but she liked Jibril's smile--something told her this was a decent young fellow, and she decided to let him off the hook, for the moment.

"Okay, but be sure to let me know if you need anything."

"Yes, Ma'am, I will, thank you," he said, grateful that she'd decided to throw him back in the water. As they sat watching *Living Single*, Jibril's urge to ask Landa who was in the picture on the wall began to build, and even though he knew it wasn't the best time, he couldn't help himself. The next thing he knew the question just popped out.

"So who's that on the wall?" he asked.

"What wall?"

"The one in the hallway."

"That's Jesus," Landa replied, with an exasperated look that said 'everybody knows that'. "Shit, I knew this boy when he was Chris, and now he be talkin' all this," she thought to herself. (If thoughts had sound he would have heard her suck her teeth.)

"Humph, that's funny," Jibril said, "somehow I thought the Bible says Jesus was Black. In fact, I thought it says that both Jesus and Moses were Black. Revelations describes Jesus as having hair "white like wool", and "feet like unto fine brass as if they burned in a furnace." Now you know who has hair like lamb's wool, and brass is already brown to begin wit', but brass burned in a furnace? C'mon. Now, I know *The Ten Commandments* had Charlton Heston playing Moses and whatnot, but in the Bible when Moses sees the burning bush, and God tells him to tell Pharaoh to let the slaves go, Moses is afraid that he won't be able to convince him. To show Moses just a little of his power, God told him to put his hand in his shirt, and according to the Bible when he took it out, "his hand was as leprous as snow," meaning it was white. It goes on to say that it turned back to what it was. Now, why would it be a miracle to turn a white man's hand white? Besides, Moses was in Egypt, and where is Egypt? Africa."

"This boy don't ever let up, do he?" Landa

thought, as she sought to move the conversation to less serious matters. "So, how's your playin' comin'?" she asked.

"It's ah-ight, it's ah-ight," was all he could muster as he tried to sound modest.

"How come you never showed me how to play?" The playful glint in her eyes as she tilted her head putting her right foot up in the chair under her stirred something in Jibril.

"I didn't know that you had any interest," was all that he could come up with.

"Well I do!" Landa offered, while weaving her neck and head round and about in exaggerated fashion with that big mischievous grin of hers.

"Well I'll show you!" He responded, mocking her tone while trying to move his head and neck likewise. When her long elegant neck weaved it was as beautiful and graceful as a swan, when his neck weaved it was as clumsy as a turkey in November running from the ax man. "Can I use this?" Jibril asked, referring to an old Ebony magazine with Whitney Houston on the cover.

"Sure," Landa said.

Rolling up the magazine like a trumpet he stood up and began to demonstrate. She laughed when she saw how he held his mouth. "No, for real that's how you have to hold your lips," he couldn't help laughing himself. "That's the only way to get the trumpet to make the sounds you want it to make."

"For real?" she asked, disbelievingly.

"For real."

141

"Why you standing all straight up, like you at attention or something?" she laughed.

"'Cause that's how you have to stand. Here, let me show you." As Landa stood her shirt rose up, revealing more of her butter soft, smooth, chocolate stomach and as Jibril's imagination saw the very edge of the outline of her breasts, he felt another hot flash radiating from the base of his spine.

Standing behind her, he made her hold the rolled up magazine with her left hand in his, up to her mouth. He placed her right hand in playing position on top of the magazine and tried to tell her how to hold her mouth. She didn't get it; so she turned her head toward his, and looking back into his face playfully pouting her lips asked, "Like this?"

At that moment, Jibril forgot how to play the trumpet. He felt another hot flash. The hardest part of his conversion, without a doubt had been the celibacy, especially since tales of romantic conquest and superhuman sexual exploits were the stuff of which legends were made around the block. Prior to his conversion he had already had a couple of girlfriends, and while he'd never managed to complete the act, he'd come awfully, awfully close a couple of times. Now, he was trying to go another way-- struggle that it was, he was trying. He'd been good so far, but as he looked at Landa's deliciously full lips, he felt himself slipping. He had already started his forward projection, when the first notes reached his ears. Who would have thought that old man Selby, Landa's next door neighbor, would have picked that moment to put on some Coltrane <u>Naima</u> (which always made Jibril think of Nsinga). The music startled Jibril, the irony and incredible timing (as if somehow the old man knew) and somehow his resolve was (for the moment) fortified by the shock. "Do you know who that is?" he asked.

"Who?" Landa asked dreamily.

"John Coltrane," he said. "He was a real deep, spiritual brotha."

As Landa watched Jibril disappear into the elevator, she had mixed emotions. She was happy that he had come by, but she could sense Hassan's impact on him. She remembered when he first changed his name. Soon after, he had verbally assaulted her when he saw her with a ham sandwich. At the time, she was still very much under her grandmother's thumb, and she just knew her grandmother would never stand for her seeing anybody affiliated with that "moozlem" stuff. Landa's grandmother was a stone-cold Georgia Baptist, and didn't play that!

As she lay in her bed that night, Landa thought about the fact that some of her friends thought that Jibril was an L7 because he wasn't clocking no crack money. True, she wanted a brotha who had something more than lint in his pocket, but she also knew that at that moment her own brother was sitting in a cell at Rikers's, having gotten busted only a month earlier. She was confused; she liked Jibril, but he intimidated her sometimes. Sometimes he was just too serious, spending hours practicing on his horn, not hanging

David Lamb

out.

Unlike the artistic dreamer Jibril seemed to be
to her, Landa's current man, Benjamin Franklin, was
to her a businessman through and through. Running
his own pharmaceutical distribution company, he was
more mature than the other young brothas she knew.
She remembered her head spinning with excitement
when he took her to Windows on the World, and
afterwards cruising through Brooklyn in his Land
Cruiser. It was certainly a step up from a movie, a Big
Mac, and a shake--and then boys had the nerve to
expect to get French-kissed after that! But not BJ, as
she, and only she, called him. No, Benjamin Franklin
was too cool to even try to kiss her that first night. To
Landa he seemed like a dream come true.

Among her circle of friends, drug dealers were
considered a "catch". She personally knew brothas as
young as fourteen who had bought their own Jeeps
(not toy jeeps either). She even knew some who had
bought the girls they went out with cars. The way she
and her crew saw it, the choice between a
"pharmacist" and a pookie wasn't hard at all--she was
going with the pharmacist. As far as Landa was
concerned, she'd rather be with a brotha who made
money off drugs than to be with one who spent all his
money on them. A brotha had to be paid in full,
period. No romance without finance. She wanted to
live large, while she was still young enough to enjoy it.

As he walked home from Landa's, Jibril
couldn't help wondering what Landa's grandmother
thought. He could still remember quite vividly

144

The Trumpet Is Blown

walking to elementary school with her serenading him,
and everyone else, as she faithfully stood on the corner
every morning singing:

Get ready for the coming of the Lord,
Yes, Jesus Christ is coming back
Get ready for the coming of the Lord, ya'll
Jesus Christ is coming back
Get ready for the coming of the Lord

He couldn't be sure if it was just his warped
memory or if he was too young to pick up any more of
the song, but it seemed that her hymn contained only
those five lines repeated over and over. At first Landa
managed to keep it hidden that the singing woman was
her grandmother, but once it came out the kids teased
her mercilessly (Jibril had gotten his jabs in too, but
even then he was kind of sweet on her, so he let up).
He hadn't seen Mrs. Root singing on the corner for
years now, and wondered if Landa's turn had stolen
her singing spirit.

Thinking about Landa's grandmother, he
couldn't help but reminisce about his own. He
laughed at how she used to torture his tender head,
wondering why it hurt when she combed it, since it
never hurt when he did. Back then, Grandma
Thomas' hair was cut in a short relaxed Afro. Her hair
seemed genuinely grateful for the opportunity to be
itself after so many years being pressed to be pressed.
Her stomach protruded somewhat over her belt line,
the extra weight reflecting the five children she'd

borne, and the unhealthy diet she'd weathered. Her
eyes had a somewhat almond shape to them, perhaps
reflecting a Native American heritage that Jibril
secretly thought she was lying about. Her voice had
a slight southern twang, most of which had been lost
in her years up North, having migrated from South
Carolina with her then-husband in the Fifties, settling
in Harlem, then the Lower East Side, and finally
Brooklyn. For years she'd been a member in good
standing at Bethany Baptist. When Jibril was a little
boy, she'd get him all dressed up in his Sunday best,
comb his hair out (despite his continuous complaints)
and take him to church with her. She'd spend much of
the time at church wrestling with him, trying to keep
him from fidgeting too much. As he got older, he
stopped fidgeting so much; instead he'd sit there trying
to dissect everything around him, the preacher's
preaching, the choir's singing, the stunning flamingo
hats, flowery wraps, everything. After the sermon, he
and the other kids would run to the back of the
church, waiting to dive into the buttery corn on the
cob, delicious macaroni salad, heavenly sweet potato
pie, fried chicken, and pig's feet. Pigs' feet--Jibril was
never really into pigs' feet, but he did love him some
bacon and some pork chops, though that seemed like
such a very long time ago.

"Lord, I just don't know what's gotten into
that boy," Grandma Thomas used to say. "First he
wants to stop eating pork and now he wants to call
himself by one of them names, bothering his poor
mother to let him change his name. Don't he know

this is America?" She'd lamented to her church sisters.

Chris expected his grandmother to be uncomfortable with his conversion, but when he first told Hassan that he wanted to convert, he was stunned and hurt by what he felt was Hassan's harsh reaction. Actually it wasn't harsh, Hassan just wanted him to be sure, he himself wanted to be sure that Chris understood what conversion meant.

"I know, Hassan, I can read, I read the stuff you gave me, and plus I've been studying on my own." He had been under Hassan's tutelage for nearly three years, and was hurt that Hassan was questioning him.

"Don't be offended young blood, I just want to be sure that you're sure," he explained. "Now the actual act of becoming a Muslim is simple. I mean, to become a Muslim, you simply need to declare your faith in Allah, and in his messenger Muhammad. We call that taking your Shahaadah. 'Laa Ilaaha Illallah, MuhammadurRasuulullah', that is: There is no deity worthy of worship but Allah, and Muhammad is the messenger of Allah. That's all, it's a simple declaration of faith. However, you need to understand that although it is a simple statement, it carries very great significance. In essence, it's as if you entered an agreement with Allah to live in accord with his will. Now you know once you sign a contract there are conditions which are required to be performed. You don't just sign on the dotted line, and that's it; well, it's the same way with Islam. Like I said, Islam is an attributive title, it describes a state of the human being, the state of one submitting to Allah's will. Now you can declare your faith, but if you're not submitting to Allah, then there's a deviation between what you say and what you do, and you're not fulfilling the terms of the contract. You understand?"

"Yeah, I understand."

Even after he'd decided to convert, it took Chris a long time to pick a new name. Hassan had assured him that he didn't have to take a new name. After all, Chris had to admit that Sharrief was named Sharrief, and he wasn't a Muslim (his mother had just liked the way it sounded). Still though, he believed in that proverb "a good name is better than gold", and he wanted to take a name that he felt fit him. Eventually he settled on Jibril. He was actually inspired by his early visits to church with his grandmother. He vaguely remembered the preacher saying something about the angel Gabriel blowing his horn, and he asked his grandmother about it. She told him that Gabriel was the archangel trumpeter of the Last Judgment. Looking through the Bible, he found that Gabriel was also responsible for the ministration of comfort and sympathy to man, and that the New Testament anointed him the herald of good tidings. Then when he turned to the Qur'an he found that it was Gabriel who was commanded to reveal the Qur'an to the Prophet. It all came together for him, the trumpet playing, his music providing comfort and sympathy, and bringing good tidings.

The Trumpet Is Blown

Chapter Twenty-seven

Like twin stereo needles, Hassan and Jibril ran circles around Boys & Girls High School track. They'd become Sunday morning fixtures there. On early Sunday mornings, a fine mist of dew rises from the grass refreshing the normally stale City air. Jibril loved waking up early on these days, basking in the calm that ascended over the projects as the rising sun painted the sky in varying tones of bright beautiful orange, yellow, and red streaks. It was as if the pharmacists and the outpatients respected some sort of Sabbath (or were just worn out from Friday and Saturday's binges). Whatever the reason, Jibril loved the calm of Sunday mornings. Compositions often came to him then--not the fiery, passionate ones that he composed between listening to gunshots, but the contemplative, melodic tunes that came to him in these moments of quiet serenity.

Jogging around the track, Hassan would often conduct pop quizzes with Jibril, naming songs and asking him to name the artist, or asking him to hum a scale until finally he'd get on Jibril's nerves and Jibril would tell him that if he really wanted to test him, to come see him on the court. Hassan had been consistently promising the young upstart that he was going to teach him a severe lesson one day. Jibril knew it was all smoke and mirrors, but Hassan talked a good game. He'd become animated, turn around and start running backwards throwing punches in combinations like Sugar Ray Robinson, brazenly warning Jibril of his impending demise on the court.

The intermittent roar of the Long Island Rail Road passing overhead would once in a while remind Jibril that he was still in the City. Eloquent church bells singing God's praises would hurry the worshipers on to morning services. Now and then an older sista who'd known Jibril since he was knee-high to an ant would pass by, resplendent in her Sunday best, and call him off the track and over to the fence where she'd marvel at how big he'd gotten and gently rebuke him for not being in Church. Today it was Mrs. Lawrence's turn. Jibril could remember her macaroni salad like it was yesterday! Just seeing her made him hungry. He wondered if she had any in the bag she had with her (maybe she'd hook him up for old time's sake, he hoped), salivating at the prospect. Back then he couldn't wait for the pastor to finish his sermon, so he could dive into a bowl of Mrs. Lawrence's macaroni. Standing in front of him in her white bonnet with its beautiful, dainty, navy bow tie and her navy dress trimmed in white, conservative black leather shoes, navy scarf, black leather gloves, and teal-colored trench coat, Mrs. Lawrence was styling.

"It's so good to see you Chris. How you been, boy?" Her oval face rounding into a smile, she bid him come over. "Come here and give Mrs. Lawrence a kiss." Jibril dragged himself over and kissed her on the cheek through the fence, trying to sneak a peak in her bag to see if she had any salad. "Your grandmother told me how well you're doing. We so proud of you." She was looking him up and down like she would look at a sapling turned tree on a return trip down south after many years absence.

"Thank you," he said, slightly embarrassed, as chiming Church bells sung in the air around them.

"Haven't seen you in church in a long time," she said, pausing for emphasis, tilting her head down, her eyes locking on Jibril, who felt them peering, probing beneath the surface. "You know," she said knowingly, with aged wisdom, "it's good to exercise your body, but you got to remember to exercise your faith too."

"I will Mrs. Lawrence," he said respectfully.

"Okay, I got to go now," she said, with an undercurrent of triumphant satisfaction, her voice rising with hope. "You take care," she said cheerfully.

"You have a good time," he called after her. He was shaking his head and smiling widely as he ran over to the area in the grass in the center of the track where Hassan was laid out stretching.

"You still owe one lap young blood."

"Sorry Charlie," Jibril said as he sat down in front of Hassan, stretching his legs out in a similar V-shaped fashion putting the soles of his white and blue Nike cross trainers up against the rubber spike bottoms of Hassan's black Adidas. "I've got my mind on other things. Boy, I'm tellin' you Hassan, that woman there, Mrs. Lawrence, she make the best'z macaroni salad you done ever had!"

"Oh I don't know, Khadija makes a mean macaroni salad in her own right." His head was cocked to the side and the pitch of his voice rose with assurance as he shook his head recalling the taste.

"Yeah, she bad, she bad, but Mrs. Lawrence. It's like this, it's like this, you claim you like basketball right?" he teased Hassan.

"Boy don't make me take you to the court!" Hassan responded with a mug on his face, as if he were Ali teasing Frazier.

"Yeah, yeah, whatever. Well it's like this, in basketball there's Michael Jordan, and then there's everyone else. Well, with macaroni salad, there's Mrs. Lawrence's, and then there's everyone else's." Hassan looked skeptical.

"Ah'm tellin' you, I was tempted to ask her if she had any with her . . ."

"C'mon . . ."

"If Ah'm lyin', Ah'm flyin. Shoot, if I wasn't so sweaty I'd go right over to that church now, sit in like when I was a little boy, wait for that sermon to be over and race them kids downstairs to the food, yes I would. Ah'm tellin' you. Mmmph, mmmph, mmmph. That's one thing about church, boy, they be throwing down on the food! Actually, it's a really nice looking church on the inside, they spend a lot on its upkeep. In fact I remember walkin' by recently and seeing that they'd replaced the front doors with some new thick oak doors. They looked really nice.

"Humph, it's weird though, the one thing that still sticks out in my mind was that statue of a bloody white Jesus hangin' behind the pastor's head over the pulpit. I don't know why, really, but even then something about that used to make me feel

152

uncomfortable. You know though, with some black people, you try to raise the issue of Jesus' blackness, and they get real defensive. They ain't tryin' to hear that."

"Well, Jibril, it's good to recognize that Jesus was black, but you know ultimately the fact that Jesus was black is only important because white people have made it an issue by forcing a white image on the world. I mean, it's like Imam Warith Deen says, 'what would happen if people sat in churches throughout the world for centuries with the image of a black man as savior of the world before them?' I remember Mario Cuomo telling this story about a young Italian priest who'd been sent to take over the parish Cuomo was attending. Now this young priest saw that his Italian and Irish parishioners were discriminating against blacks, so he asked them how they could discriminate when the very church they were sitting in, 'Santa Monica', was named after an African woman who was St. Augustine's mother. Now do you know that instead of reexamining their behavior these people moved to another parish? Which says to me that they were more concerned with white affirmation, than they were with being good Christians."

David Lamb

Chapter Twenty-eight

Hassan was so happy that Jibril was finally in the studio, his face glowed proudly as he spoke.

"This is a tremendous, tremendous opportunity Jibril. Do you realize that in its short history Jazz Ahead has showcased, promoted, and placed some of the finest new young Jazz talent? That young trumpet player, Peven Everett, landed a gig with Branford Marsalis' band after appearing in Jazz Ahead. You could be next! Roy Hargrove picked up his drummer Karriem Riggins there. Now listen to me Jibril, you can play as well as any of these cats and you've got what Betty Carter is looking for. Hey? What's that look?"

"What look?"

"That look, that look of doubt."

"I don't know, I mean those guys were a little older than me."

"*That* doesn't matter. Believe me, Jibril, I wouldn't lie to you. It's your moment, it's your time. You've got the technical proficiency, you've got the chops, plus you've got the emotional depth and the spiritual vision. You could do for the trumpet what Coltrane did for the sax!"

"Oh c'mon now! Now you're gassin' me."

"Okay I got a little carried away," Hassan agreed, with a sheepish grin that belied his five decades. "But seriously, Ah'm telling you, you've got what she wants."

"How do you know? How do you know what

154

she wants?"

"Because I spoke to her, and I asked her what she was looking for."

"And she said me!" Jibril deadpanned sarcastically.

"In so many words that's exactly what she said. She said she takes musicians from all over. She visits colleges to hear what's happening there. Then she listens to young cats people have told her about. She'll even consider unsolicited tapes--at least listen to them. She told me that everyone who comes to her she listens to how they keep time, how they handle rhythm, can they swing a solo, how they're trying to create. She also listens to how developed their chops are--not that their playing has to be perfect; after all, most of you cats are so young, but she believes they've got to have feeling in their chops. Most of all, she wants them to be themselves. She doesn't want anyone's style but theirs. She understands that you should know the styles that came before you, but you've got to be developing your own voice. That's paramount. That's how I knew that she'd love you, because those are exactly the qualities I look for, and those I've tried to encourage you to develop. She said when she heard you, she knew."

"When she heard me?"

"Well, I wasn't going to tell you this," Hassan teased.

"Tell me what? Tell me, tell me!" Jibril demanded impatiently, hoping for such high-placed praise and confirmation.

"She said that she knew . . ."

"Knew what?"

"Knew that you had that special--that indescribable something. 'Something that you just feel inside,' she said. She knew right away."

Beaming with pride and brimming with confidence from Hassan's good news, Jibril floated into the studio with Louis, Dizzy, Clifford, Miles, Lee, Freddie, Terry, and Wynton all whispering words of encouragement. He flawlessly blew through all the styles. And then, to Hassan's surprise, made his own original musical statement, playing for the first time publicly (except for his visit to his brother's grave), his statement of musical arrival. Hassan was quite literally blown away, and gently allowed himself a brief smile. "Job well done," a little voice whispered to him.

The Trumpet Is Blown

Chapter Twenty-nine

"Aw man, Bilal, yo', I saw Landa the other night. Damn!" Jibril exclaimed as he collapsed against his mother's deep blue couch still wrapped safely by plastic.

"*Shehadonthishortpinkshirtcutoffat'thebelly, I was likesweating, youknowwhatah'msayin'*," he was talking so fast his words were running together.

"Yo' what's up wit' that? What about Nsinga?" Jibril responded with an annoyed frown.

He felt like he didn't really need Bilal to remind him of Nsinga; his feelings for her ran well beyond physical attraction. It was, he felt, as though they were meant to be together. Years before, Nsinga would sit, unbeknownst to Jibril and Hassan, at the top of the stairs leading to the basement, listening warmly to Jibril rehearse, his playing stirring feelings she couldn't explain. No one else had ever made her feel that way. On the days he was supposed to come over she would sit at the kitchen table anxiously watching the clock, feverishly counting down the minutes to his arrival. One day Jibril arrived early. Khadija told him he could wait downstairs. Sitting at the kitchen table, Nsinga strained to hear him play. Her mother asked her to ask Jibril if he wanted any lemonade. She ran down the steps as quickly as she could, and then stopped and dreamily watched him stroke the keys, unaware of her presence. She softly sighed. At the sound of the sigh, Jibril turned and saw her smile brightening the room. Yes. Yes, he would like some lemonade. Nsinga ran back up the steps as quickly as she could. Running back even faster. That day she didn't sit at the top of the stairs. While Jibril practiced, she sat at the stair's base, staring with the innocent fawning of first love. Feeling her eyes on him, Jibril couldn't concentrate--he was trying not to blush. Finally, Hassan arrived and she ran back upstairs to greet him. After that day, Jibril would periodically arrive a little early, hoping that Hassan wouldn't be there. It was as if he and Nsinga had some unwritten pact. She would sit at the base of the stairs watching him run through scales; he couldn't face her when he played otherwise he'd smile and be unable to play. Every now and then, he'd take a peak over his shoulder, and turn back quickly before the bursting smile on his face embarrassed him. Sometimes she would imagine that he was teaching her to play, gently guiding her fingers with his fingers across the keys, punching out notes and tunes that serenaded their blossoming love, but then Hassan would arrive and she'd go back upstairs.

"I know man. You know she's got my heart," Jibril confessed. "I don't even really like Landa as a person, but something about her, I got to admit, when I see her, I be like losin' it. I don't know what to do. I tried to pray on it, but I didn't want to pray about something like that, you know, but then I couldn't even pray if I wanted to 'cause I couldn't concentrate 'cause I had her hips on my mind."

"Yeah, I know what you mean, it's like you be tryin' to keep yourself in check, but yo', hey, that's the hardest thing. I mean, I ain't got no taste for forties and blunts, but sistas! I remember this older brotha telling me one time that a beautiful woman will make a man put down the Qur'an. I didn't know what he meant, you know, I was tryin' to picture it--literally, somebody sittin' there readin' the Qur'an and Naomi Campbell comes walkin' by and the brotha's fightin' it, but he can't help himself. So, I kicked it wit' him a little bit, and he explained how he was just speakin' metaphorically. What he was sayin', he said, was that in our pursuit of satisfyin' that desire that we'll ofttimes be willin' to sacrifice our principles. Then he looked me in the eyes, all serious like, and said to me, 'remember, women come and go, but Allah remains.'"

"Damn, women come and go, but Allah remains."

"Yep, so I try and remember that. I mean, I'm not tryin' to say I don't ever go astray, but that's why Allah is oft-returning to mercy, 'cause human beings are constantly slippin' up."

"Ain't that the truth."

Sometimes, listening to Jibril rehearse, Nsinga would sit cross-legged, her back supported by the bed, her palms flat and outstretched against the wooden floor. She would rest her head back, listening to Jibril blow, close her eyes, see the colors and feel the sounds. Listening warmly to Jibril rehearse, Nsinga would be enveloped by the hypnotic, hauntingly beautiful timbre of the horn's wail, the sound filling her, embracing her, carrying her breath away. Gently swaying to the rhythmic melody invading her soul and impelling her to sculpt; caressing the clay, molding and shaping the form in harmony with the music encapsulating her world. Like her favorite sculptor, Elizabeth Catlett, Nsinga's art was shaped by her political views. Like Catlett, she used expressionistic and distorting techniques to capture and stir the imagination. Her favorite Catlett work was <u>The Black Woman Speaks</u>. She tried to incorporate the characteristic Catlett upward tilt of the head into her work, because she thought it so ennobling. She dreamed of the day when one of her works would adorn university campuses the way Catlett's has. She indelibly etched the image of Catlett's Louis Armstrong monument in her mind, creating in her inner vision a similar work honoring Marcus Garvey that would one day embellish Marcus Garvey Park in Harlem the way Satchmo's visage enhanced the New Orleans park named in his honor. When she looked at the Prison Ship Martyrs Monument in Fort Green Park, first built in 1908 commemorating the American Revolutionaries who died on board English prison ships in Wallabout Bay, she imagined a similar monument acknowledging the horrors of the Middle Passage and celebrating the desire of Africa's descendants to regain that which they'd lost. She envisioned two ships, one crossing through turbulent seas to America and one, bearing the crest of Garvey's Black Star Line, gliding along placid waters toward West Africa. This, she thought, would truly honor the spirit of Garvey.

In her paintings, Nsinga tried to emulate the

The Trumpet Is Blown

style of Lois Mailou Jones. It was in studying Jones' style that she discovered the African inspiration behind Picasso's Cubism. Like Jones, Nsinga had an affinity for bright colors, and in her own way tried to incorporate Jones' interweaving of African masks and textiles into her work. What really drew her to Jones was the center stage black women took in her art, which in unique and beautiful ways depicted young women coming of age.

Sometimes Nsinga would make them pose for hours, or so it felt to Jibril and Bilal who would complain endlessly the whole time. How she was able to keep her concentration in the face of their ceaseless playful gestures and gimmicks sometimes amazed even her. Nsinga hadn't realized that she had any artistic ability until she was forced to sculpt a mask as part of her seventh grade art class. Her talent was immediately apparent. When her art teacher called Khadija, at first her mother thought that Nsinga had been acting up, but before the onslaught of her teacher's profuse praise she learned that her daughter had an abundance of theretofore undiscovered potential. Khadija and Hassan encouraged the bud of Nsinga's talents to flower, turning a walk-in closet into a little art studio where she would ultimately turn out stunningly beautiful and thought-provoking works.

The Trumpet Is Blown

Chapter Thirty

Shaun knew that he had to do something else with his life. When he looked around there wasn't anybody in his whole crew older than twenty-two, so it was clear to him that there wasn't any future in the game. As Jibril walked past him on his way to school that morning, they nodded to each other, each wondering what was going to become of the other.

"Yo' man, why you talkin' 'bout gettin' out the game?" Mic-Boogie asked Shaun, before taking a swig of his freshly cracked St. Ides. "Believe me, I know how it is to get up feelin' all guilty and shit, tired of people lookin' at you like it's all your fault that niggaz like crack more than salt, but what the fuck else a nigga gonna do? Man, in Bed Stuy a nigga either sellin' crack rock or got a deadly jump shot, and I know your ass can't play ball. So what the fuck? Man, whenever I feel that guilt shit creeping up I jus' remember my moms being broke as hell, grab me a forty and a shorty, and think about when Ah'm off the block, livin' lovely. Be like Special Ed and buy a tiny isle of my very own! Word, or be like that nigga AZ puffin' cheeba in Costa Rica wit' a fly honey who knows how to treat ya, *youknowwhatah'msayin'*," he declared enthusiastically before topping it off with an emphatic pound.

"Yeah, whatever," Shaun said before drowning his thoughts in a flood of malt liquor. Ignorance is bliss, he was thinking. Too bad for him he had too much sense to see that 'the life' was death. He

David Lamb

couldn't bask in the arrogance of ignorance. In his world he was alone--the others just didn't get it, they really thought that they had it made. He remembered trying to talk to Mic-Boogie before. When he was bragging about how much money he was making, Shaun asked him how much he was making an hour. He tried to make him see, the way Jibril had tried to make him see, that by the time he counted in the bad nights, the nights the police wouldn't let them work, the nights spent in jail, the slow, thunderstorm-filled evenings when even the pookies stayed inside, the blistering, freezing, long winter nights, the ducking from rivals, they couldn't possibly be making more than nine dollars an hour, tops. "For this? For this?!" he asked rhetorically. "I don't know, man, I don't know if it's worth it."

"You crazy, what else you gonna do that lets you get the honeys, the cars, the gear? Nigga please, stop whining."

When Shaun looked into the future, it wasn't a pretty picture.

Wiping the sleep from his half-closed eyes, Jibril looked through the peephole and saw Shaun anxiously pacing back and forth. His clothes were drenched from the downpour and he didn't even have an umbrella or a hoodie. The water running down his face made him look as if he'd been crying.

"Yo', wussup man! Why you knockin' on my door so late?"

"Yo' I need to talk to you." Shaun's serious

164

The Trumpet Is Blown

tone alarmed and awakened Jibril.

"About what?"

"Yo' I just need to talk, can I please come in?"
Shamed by Shaun's humility and torn by the image of
this shattered shell of his friend, Jibril acquiesced.

"Yeah, man, come in. What's up?"

"Yo' man, I just need to talk, I'm feelin' all
effed up."

"What's up, man?"

"Man, you don't know, man. The shit that
goes down. Remember Lakesha?"

"Yeah, you kidding, of course." Jibril couldn't
help smiling recalling how beautiful Lakesha was.

"Remember, man? Remember we both had a
crush on her back in the fourth grade, used to write
her love letters and shit, slip them under her door and
knock and run? Man, you couldn't tell me I wasn't in
love."

"Me, either."

"I can remember it so clearly, going into
assembly, I'd be so happy when I'd walk down the
aisle next to her. Damn! But, man, shit's all fuck'd up
now."

"What are you talkin' 'bout, man?" His
anxious voice was deep and he slowed his speech
purposely.

"Man, not three days ago, I saw her."

"For real?! I haven't seen her in a century."

"Man, not three days ago she comes in the
spot. She was all skinny and stinkin' and shit, her eyes
and teeth were all yellow. Remember how fine she

165

was? She recognizes me, and offers to 'slob the knob' for some crack. That fuck'd me up, you know, 'cauz I remembered how she used to be, so I told her to go home and clear her head. Man, don't you know she cursed me out. Then buffed Mic-Boogie's helmet right in front of me, no condom, no nothing. That shit fucked me all the way up! That's why I know I'm going to hell."

"Shaun, now you know you my man. You know, me and you go back like vertebrae, to quote my man Treach," he laughed, "and you know, even though I didn't like it at the time, I really appreciate the fact that you tried to talk some sense into me when I was tryin' to get a gun, so now I wanna return the favor if I can, *knowwhatI'msayin'*. Now, the way I see it, brotha, on the real," his voice filling with sincerity, he continued, "you already in hell, and the only way out is to make a change. Our situation, yours and mine, black people in America, is not going to change unless we change. Now, let's be real. Look how foul we livin'--most of us just chillin', sippin' 40s, puffin' lye, tryin' to skeez, *youknowwnatah'msayin'*. We like that, no responsibility, just chillin', slangin' when a sale comes along, gat strapped for the rep. We like living foul, and as long as we feel comfortable livin' foul we gonna keep livin' foul, so the only way we're gonna change is if our foul lifestyle ain't chill no more--if the way we're livin' brings about nothing but death and destruction on our heads, then we'll start lookin' for a way out."

The Trumpet Is Blown

If this had been anyone else talking to him like he was being spoken to Shaun would have told them to go to hell a long time ago, but it was true, even though they weren't that close anymore, they went way back, and Shaun still loved Jibril like a brother, and he knew that Jibril likewise loved him. Shaun knew that Jibril was only telling him the truth. Deep down he admired Jibril, and wanted to be more focused like him, go back to school, turn his life around, make his mother and his son proud of him. But getting out the game was so hard, and the consequences frightened him.

"Now, personally I believe that you're a good brotha, deep down--real deep", Jibril said with a smile. "And potentially the smartest person I've ever met, besides me of course." (He couldn't help the sarcasm.) "You just don't wanna change, but I'm tellin' you until you make up your mind that you're gonna get out the game and change your life, then misery and woe are gonna be your homeboys. It's like this, remember when we were little and we walked all the way to that store just to steal some baseball cards, and then had the nerve to get caught?"

"Yeah, that was some funny shit. You tried to put them in your umbrella and walk out."

"Yeah, I was buggin'," a laughing Jibril reminisced. "It was in May, on a sunny day, no rain in a week and I walk in wit' an umbrella."

"Yeah, you just didn't have the criminal mind," Shaun said, while chuckling at the memory.

"Yeah, ah-ight whatever, but anyway, this is

167

serious."

"Okay, okay," Shaun agreed.

"It's like I was sayin', when we got caught, your moms had to come get us and she whipped that ass good, right? Damn, she tore you up now that I recall it," he said, with a chuckle. "Then remember that other time when we were real young and almost fell into the river after wandering off at that picnic and my moms caught us and lectured us about wandering off. You remember that, right?"

"Yeah."

"Well, in both cases, the aim was the same, to get us to change our behavior for the better. It's like I heard Farrakhan say, sometimes the way to get a message to the mind--is through the ear, but other times the way to get a message to the mind is through the behind--different methods, same objective. Check it out, check it out, right, you seen *The Ten Commandments,* right?"

"True dat. True dat." A clicking of his tongue signified that Shaun had indeed seen the Cecil B. DeMilles epic.

"Well, Moses tried to change Pharaoh's heart by speakin' to him, but Pharaoh was too arrogant, he wasn't tryin' to hear that, he was the Man! He was all that! Livin' phat, it was all good! Well, just like Pharaoh, a lot a brothas sellin' drugs think that they're so large that they become arrogant, and won't listen to anybody tryin' to tell them to do right. They ain't tryin' to hear that, like the Qur'an says 'they turn their backs proudly . . . as if there were deafness in [their] ears.' They be like, 'yeah, nigga, step off, before I bust a cap in yo' ass,' *youknowwhatah'msayin'*. So that's when Allah's got to whip out that belt, and start tearin' that ass up. You see what happened to Pharaoh, plagues started hittin', and he still wouldn't change, until finally Allah had to take him out! Same thing today--look how that nigga Priest ended up stabbed to death in some stinking ass jail cell by one of his own dope fiends!

"So, yo', not to be cold, just real honest--I'm glad to see that you're suffering, because it's makin' you think about the way you livin'. And I hope that you start thinkin' about livin' a new way. As cold as this might sound, the best thing that might ever have happened to Mike Tyson was going to jail on that rape conviction, 'cauz it forced him to look at how he was livin', the hell that he was bringin' upon his own self, and to make a change. All I'm sayin' to you, brotha, is be like Mike and make a change."

"Yeah, I hear you, but I don't know how to do anything else. I mean, I'm not like you, I don't play an instrument, and I can't play ball."

The Trumpet Is Blown

Chapter Thirty-one

Before the brothers organized by the Mosque actually began their patrol, they decided to organize an anti-drug demonstration in order to rally community support for the patrol. They made up flyers announcing the day and time, and reached out to local churches, community groups, and small business owners. Although the police were still skeptical of the idea of a patrol, they nevertheless donated a bullhorn and megaphone for the rally, and agreed to close off the street. Benjamin was extremely agitated because the rally was being held on the day he did his best volume--Thursday--the day City workers were paid.

Down the block, the marchers marched singing: 'Down wit' Dope, Up wit' Hope!' They chanted rhythmically in a tone that was simultaneously serious and lighthearted. They marched up to a grandstand that had been set up. Throughout the day various speakers denounced drugs and called on the City to do more.

"Now listen," Imam Aziz began, "life is not meant to be lived in fear. If we have to be afraid to leave our homes, to walk down our blocks, then something is terribly wrong in Bedford-Stuyvesant. We called this rally together because we want the dealers to know their day is done. Down wit' dope, up wit' hope!" he roared to the crowd's delight.

"Hope for a brighter tomorrow where our wives, our husbands, and our children can walk the streets without fear of gunfire. Where our mothers

171

can walk without fear of being mugged. Down wit' dope, up wit' hope. Hope for a new day, when the crack house will be replaced by the school house. Hope for a day when our young men and women, rather than aspiring to be drug dealers, will go on to college and become real pharmacists and chemical engineers. Down wit' dope, up wit' hope! Hope that our sons and daughters will grow up in a society where they have real hope in a promising future. The hope is in our hands, if we say no, the dealer's gotta go. If we say no, the dealer's gotta go. If we say no . . ."

The Trumpet Is Blown

Chapter Thirty-two

"Yo', J-Son, bust it, Ah'm thinkin' 'bout changin' my name," Mic-Boogie said enthusiastically.

"Word? To what?" J-Son asked.

"Feloni."

"*Feloni?*"

"Word, Feloni, like baloney."

"Feloni, hmm, that shit is dope, kid," J-Son said, impressed by the unique sound of the name.

"What's it mean?"

"I think it's Italian for felony." Mic-Boogie responded, smiling at his own creative genius.

"Yo', that shit is the bomb, son. Ain't no niggaz out here got no name like dat."

"True dat, true dat." Mic-Boogie's head bobbed up and down triumphantly as he spoke.

"Yo', but you was sayin' that nigga Benjamin is swift callin' the cops on them Muslim mugs! Yo', how'd he think'a that, son?" J-Son asked in admiration, as he squatted comfortably on his standard perch at the top of the crumbling stairs leading into the Lab.

"*Youknowwhatah'msayin'*, that's like, it's like some, but yo', you know, stuff like that, word, *youknowwhatah'msayin'*. Straight up, they don't want no parts of this, *youknowwhatah'msayin'*, on the real, *youknowwhatah'msayin'*," Mic-Boogie elaborated in his own uniquely indecipherable manner, before taking a swig of his morning St. Ides.

173

"Yo', what up wit' them crab ass niggaz anyway?"

"Yo' niggaz was lookin' at a nigga sideways when he was rollin' by. Them cartoon niggaz don't know a nigga like me a act like a nigga, *youknowwhatah'msayin', wordemup!* Them Muslim niggaz better act like they know, comin' wit' that karate chop chop they bound to get shot. *Youknowwhatah'msayin'.*" An animated Mic-Boogie demonstrated as he grabbed the bulge under his shirt.

"Yeah, you know Ah'm down for whatever whatever."

"So how he plan on pulling this shit off?"

"Yo', bust it right, check it out, that nigga gonna wait 'til Friday afternoon when them niggaz is in church, and he gonna call up and say that there's somebody in there wit' a gun holdin' mu'fuckas hostage and shit." His sinister laugh confirmed Mic-Boogie's admiration of the seeming sheer genius of Benjamin's deviousness.

"Yo' that's like some of that 'ol next shit. You think that's a good idea?" a concerned J-Son asked, peering over his shoulder.

"Yo' he the boss, whatever that nigga say go. Besides I think that shit is a dope idea!"

"I jus' hope that shit don't backfire."

"It won't," Mic-Boogie said confidently.

The Trumpet Is Blown

Chapter Thirty-three

Nsinga was surprised by how quickly she'd learned the three Chinese love songs. She, Bilal, Carlos, and Jibril had been practicing ever since Jimmy Chin had hired the band, and she really couldn't wait to sing at the wedding.

Much to his neighbor's chagrin, Jibril had been practicing the high-pitched intonations of Chinese music. Unfortunately, as much as he'd practiced, he still didn't know if he was good or bad, and he wasn't sure how the crowd would react.

Even Bilal, who was a nonbelieiver at first, had been experimenting with how to make his cymbals sound like traditional Chinese gongs.

The wedding hall they were about to play in was huge--intimidatingly so, and was beautifully decorated with red curtains with gold-colored Chinese writing.

They were all nervous when it came time to perform.

Nsinga cleared her throat one last time, imagining in her mind's eye a perfectly performed solo.

At the end of the first song, the hall was as silent as a muted television. A grim-faced, yet smiling (forced smile that it was) Jimmy Chin walked up to the stage, looking dashing in his custom-fitted tux.

Jibril, like everyone else on stage, was confused. Did they like it? Did they hate it? Jimmy had his back to the crowd as he whispered to Jibril, "I thought you a Jazz musician."

"I am," Jibril replied, as Bilal strained to hear what was being said.

"Then why aren't you playing Jazz?"

Jibril was dumbfounded, and feebly responded, "But it's a Chinese wedding!"

Jimmy looked at him as if Jibril were stupid, and said, "So, Chinese people can't like Jazz?"

"Oops," Jibril whispered.

"Now play us some music," Jimmy said, as he turned to the crowd and apologized for the interruption, still smiling that forced smile.

"All right ya'll from the top," Jibril said as Nsinga, Carlos, and Bilal looked on in confusion. "Nsinga, afraid there ain't gonna be no singin' today, so warm up your piano fingers. Okay, here we go, we'll start wit' High Modes then go into Night In Tunisia."

In the audience, Jimmy smiled. "Now that's more like it," he said.

The Trumpet Is Blown

Chapter Thirty-four

Like the increasingly thunderous roar of an approaching train, the commotion slowly rose from somewhere beyond Hassan's vision. Like the notes of a soaring Satchmo solo, figures rose and fell as the violent twirling of batons parted the sea of worshipers. Dramatic angry cries of protest could be heard as the batons' drumming grew ever more violent. Despite watching his diet, in spite of his steady diet of exercise, Hassan was not a young man anymore. Still, he rose in protest--and then he fell.

Jibril hated going to the hospital. He detested the smell, the squeaky floors, the constant deluge of nearly unintelligible voices battling for attention over the hospital's speaker system. He'd spent too much time in hospitals when he was a little boy. First, he'd gotten hit by a car while chasing a ball into the street. Soon after, his asthma attacks began. He never knew if there was a logical, medical connection, but it seemed that right after coming home from his overnight stay that the asthma attacks began. Before he knew it, he was an emergency room regular. He could still remember his mother rubbing his hand as he lay encapsulated in his protective oxygen tank; he couldn't have been more than five or six years old at the time. He remembered one night in particular when his mother frantically rushed him to the hospital worried because his skin had dried and flaked from the lack of oxygen. After a while, the hospital didn't seem half bad to him--there had been something perversely cool about being sick. When he came home all his little friends and family would be so happy to see him because he'd been away. He got to miss school. It actually seemed all right.

Jibril hadn't had an asthma attack in years. He was sure he'd outgrown it, yet being back in the hospital made him uneasy. It wouldn't be cool, perversely or otherwise, to be hospitalized now. Jibril hated going to the hospital. He remembered going to see Bilal's older brother as he wasted away from AIDS-induced pneumonia. He remembered being there the night his homeboy Keith got stabbed. He remembered being there the morning his friend, Darnell, got shot. It seemed to him that hospitals were less a place for healing and more a morgue and a mourning place for the too young to die.

"How's he doing?"

"The doctor said that he's going to be fine, but you know what a big baby he is, he likes all the attention," Nsinga said, trying to make light of a serious matter. "Go on in, he'll be happy to see you."

Jibril wasn't used to seeing him this way, he'd always been so strong. Now, seeing him lying in a hospital bed shook up Jibril. Instantly sensing the despair on Jibril's face, Hassan tried to cheer him up.

"Hey, little brother, glad to see you could finally make it," he said sarcastically. "Where's your trumpet? I know you don't think you're getting out of today's lesson that easily," he said with a faint chuckle, which drew a similarly faint smile from Jibril.

The Trumpet Is Blown

"So how you feeling, man?" Jibril asked, with obvious concern.

"Ah'm all right, can't keep a good man down," he managed to respond through a sudden, loud racking cough, before Khadija came in and gently told Jibril that visiting hours were almost over.

In the corridor outside Hassan's room, Jibril sought out Nsinga for an explanation. The story he'd first heard sounded so bizarre to him that he had to check it out.

"So what really happened? I heard some crazy story about the police busting in the mosque. What went down?"

"It's true, right in the middle of the Imam's khutbah, around twenty cops came bursting through the Masjid. They trampled through with no respect, kept their muddy shoes on, stepping on worshipers, pushing people. At first, there was just mass confusion--people were screaming, you could hear bone being struck by batons, nobody knew what was happening. Then about four or five cops pushed their way to the front and grabbed the Imam--right in the middle of his sermon--threw him down and tried to handcuff him. Some of the brothers tried to jump in and protect him. The police took out their batons and beat them off, and then a couple of the cops started spraying that pepper spray. My father took a full blast in the face. He had an allergic reaction, and it triggered an asthma attack and he had to be rushed to the hospital. When I got the message at school, I was so upset, I didn't know what to do, I just came

David Lamb

straight here." As the tears welled up in her eyes, Nsinga's body shook with emotion. Jibril put his arm around her shoulder and promised her that everything would be all right. It had to be. He hated hospitals.

He recalled his first time being in a mosque. What struck him most was the lack of music--there was no organ, no choir. He remembered taking off his shoes as he went to join the other worshipers. The floor was carpeted in sumptuous deep green, while white ceiling fans with gold colored blades spun from above providing light relief from the oppressive summer heat. There were three large semicircle-shaped windows on two sides and these were encapsulated by green and gold wooden shudders. He could still recall quite vividly the first time he heard Hassan call the believers to prayer. There was something musical about it, almost bluesy, as his bassy voice and captivating phrasing reached into the very depths of Jibril's soul filling his breath with faith.

The Trumpet Is Blown

Chapter Thirty-five

"It's hard to believe that they were actually going to arrest me for resisting arrest. Thanks for intervening, Charlie," Hassan said.

"Hey, that's what I'm here for. I'm just glad you're back home and finally out of the hospital. So how are you feeling?"

"Oh, I'm fine, I'm fine."

"Really?"

"Really, I am. You know, it's really ironic though, if this whole affair had never happened we would never have gotten such police support. All this time they've been opposing the Imam's efforts to establish a patrol, and now they're acting like they thought it up in the first place."

"Well, you know, the precinct captain was so embarrassed about his men's behavior. It's all over the news, and now they're just trying to do damage control." Charlie always saw the political angle, and this situation was no different.

"Well, I say let's take advantage of it." Then after a pause, Hassan laughed slyly and said, "Besides we can always sue them later."

"Well, I'm just glad you're okay," Charlie said sincerely. "Are you sure that you want to go through with this?"

"Yeah, I'm sure," Hassan concluded.

David Lamb

Chapter Thirty-six

"We know that what we're undertaking involves great danger," Imam Aziz said solemnly, pausing to take a deep breath and look into the eyes of those assembled before him in the Mosque's basement. "But it would be even more dangerous to not do anything. Prophet Muhammad, peace be upon him, advised us that when we see an injustice we should stop it with our hands, meaning we should physically intervene. He was pragmatic; however, he knew that we would not always be in a position to physically intervene, so he said that if we could not stop it with our hands, then stop it with our tongue, meaning speak out against injustice and oppression. But he knew that there would be times that we wouldn't even be able to do that, so he said, if we cannot speak out, then we should protest it in our hearts. This is the weakest of faith--it's still faith, but it doesn't require the same level of commitment as physically intervening or speaking out. It takes faith, and our faith is built through prayer, our discipline is built through the five daily prayers, our faith and discipline are built through fasting. These things we do, giving zakat, giving away our hard-earned money for the support of the community, having faith that Allah will reward us for what we give.

"It takes faith, man." Clasping his hands and pausing, the Imam let his point sink in. Those gathered before him had volunteered to patrol the streets risking life and limb and he wanted to be sure that they understood the danger--wanted to be sure that they were firm in their resolve. "It takes faith to stand up to oppression, this is why we find in the Qur'an that Moses, before going to face Pharaoh beseeched Allah to increase him in faith. That's what it means when it says that he prayed to Allah to 'expand his breast'. Nowadays we would say, 'give him some heart', some courage. And that is what you and I must pray for if we are to go out there and face down this menace. We must pray for courage, because believe me, brothers, we will be tested. Allah tells us in the Qur'an that we will be tested, but let's face this challenge with courage.

"When we go out, those young brothas are not just going to disappear. In their eyes, we're threatening their livelihood. Just imagine if someone were to come down to your job, and tell you that you couldn't work there anymore? Imagine how outraged you'd feel and how you'd automatically want to respond. If we hold fast, though, and keep the faith and vigilance, we will be victorious."

Imam Abdul-Aziz Omowale was a man of quiet charisma and dignity. He stood six feet tall with a medium build--not muscular, but toned, and much more athletic than men his age tended to be. He was a man not prone to violence and not one at first glance that you would imagine challenging crack dealers face to face, but on closer inspection, his eyes revealed a calm resolve and faith in his maker come what may. The kind of faith, Charlie Stokes saw, that inspired others to follow his lead. Heck, Charlie himself was

David Lamb

inspired.

The first time Imam Aziz heard the words "Allah-u-Akbar (God is Greater)", he was in prison in Virginia. He was just nineteen years old, and had broken into the local liquor store with some of his boys. He didn't know anything about being a Muslim--in fact, had never heard the word before. All of that changed one night at dinner. The menu consisted of pork chops, mashed potatoes, carrots, a glass of milk, and a glass of apple juice. He heard one brotha ask for an extra helping of carrots because the brotha said that he didn't eat pork, so he didn't want any pork chops. When he said that, all within earshot perked up. (Because everyone knew all black folk loved pork!) The white prisoner serving the food gave him an extra helping of pork chops instead of giving him extra carrots, so all he had was an extra helping of pork chops, and some mashed potatoes. The brotha said respectfully, "Sir, Ah'm sorry you must have misunderstood me. I said that I would like an extra helping of carrots and *no* porkchops, please." The server ignored him and started serving the next guy in line, so the brotha repeated himself only this time in a little louder, but still polite tone. Then the guy serving the food called the guards over and told them that the brotha was causing trouble. The brotha responded very calmly that he didn't eat pork, and when they heard that, one of the guards got all red in the face. He must have known that the brotha was a Muslim, or maybe he just thought he was 'uppity'. Whatever he thought, he responded hostilely, "Well, nigger, you're

184

going to eat pork tonight." At that, the brotha just turned and walked away leaving his tray behind. The guard called after him, "Hey! Hey boy! You hear me talking to you. Come get this food, boy!" As the brotha stopped and stood in his tracks, another guard picked up the plate and brought it to him. "I said take your plate boy!" he shouted.

"Sir, I am no longer hungry," the brotha said.

"Well, you didn't make my partner carry this tray all the way over here for nothing did you boy?" The brotha was silent, everybody was watching! By this time, the second guard had his blackjack out and ready. Suddenly, he struck the brotha full in the stomach.

"Answer me when I'm talking to you boy!"

"I'm not hungry sir," the brotha managed between coughs. The guard commenced to whomping on the brotha's skull. The brotha swung in some sort of martial arts move, grabbed the guard's arm, brought it down over his knee and forced him to let the blackjack go. By then, about eight guards had gathered around, but they didn't know what to do, they just looked at each other. Then the guard whose blackjack had been forced out of his hands, rushed at the brotha from his knees, grabbed his legs and started biting him, so hard that he actually drew blood. The brotha screamed in pain and the other guards were on him in an instant-- beating him and force feeding him the porkchops right there in front of everybody, but he still would not eat. And the whole time he kept shouting out words that seemed strange to the future

David Lamb

Imam's ears. "Allah-u-Akbar, Allah-u-Akbar!" The Imam didn't know what to think. An older prisoner saw his mouth gaping open and whispered to him, "That cat's a moozlem." He decided he was going to talk to him about this moozlem stuff. Had to talk to him.

The Trumpet Is Blown

Chapter Thirty-seven

"I remember one day when I was eleven, and I was hungry as a muthafucka. Man, I looked at my little brother and he was all dirty and shit, you know. I went to my mom's for some money, but her stupid ass had spent all the money on crack. That's why, and I never told nobody this before," he said, before casting a silent stern glance at Glock to emphasize that this was just between them. "But that's why I never let mu'fuckas accept food stamps, I know what that shit is like, bitch got a baby at home, and instead of buying baby food she's using the shit for crack, fuck that! That's that bitch's problem. If she need money, she need to sell that ass or something, but don't be depriving the baby, *knowwhatah'msayin'*." This was the first time Benjamin Franklin had ever discussed his love/hate relationship with his mother to anyone, and he was practically shaking with fury. Looking out the window of his sparsely-furnished (most of his money went to clothes) second-floor apartment, Benjamin kept an eye on his workers while recounting for Glock's enjoyment his rapid rise in 'the Business'.

"So, anyway, Homeboy had offered me seventy-five bones to be a lookout for three hours, *shit,* twenty-five dollars an hour, as hungry and desperate as I *was.* So, I went and looked out for Five-Oh, none showed, three hours later, that nigga was counting off seventy-five dollars in my hand. I ran home and got my little brother and we went to that

David Lamb

Kentucky Fried joint on the Ave. Yo' them mu'fuckas in Kentucky looked at us like we was buggin', but I didn't give a fuck. We had a whole bucket of extra-crispy between us, we was throwin' down, faces all greasy and shit." Glock couldn't help but notice Benjamin's joy as he recalled his first encounter with the power of money--one day's work and he was able to keep hunger at bay and feed himself and his little brother. Glock smiled, imagining Benjamin's greasy face happily buried in a giant bucket of Kentucky Fried.

"Yo' what's up wit' your brother? I ain't seen that nigga in a long while." Benjamin's response, a deadly cold glare, told Glock not to ask about his brother anymore.

As far as Benjamin was concerned, his younger brother was a traitor. After all he'd done for him! After all he'd done for him. "That nigga, of all niggaz, had the nerve to start talkin' that Muslim shit," Benjamin thought. Last he'd heard his brother was living with some family in Atlanta. "Fuck that nigga," Benjamin said to himself. "Yo' after that it was on," Benjamin continued with increased enthusiasm, *"knowwhatah'msayin'*, I looked out for that nigga the day after that, got me another seventy-five--I still had forty from the day before stashed. I wanted to get some Jordans, but I needed more money, so the next day I looked out for that nigga again, got me another seventy-five bones and a pair of Jordans, but then I look down at my little brother and his ass was still just as raggedy, so next thing I knew I was out there again.

The Trumpet Is Blown

Shit, now I was used to that seventy-five. I was doing it every day after school. It was the wintertime and it was starting to get real cold outside. I was snifflin' and shakin' and shit, 'cauz my little piece of coat wasn't making it, but I was out there every day anyway, and soon I had enough to buy me and my little brother new coats.

"I was learnin' the game fast though, out there keepin' watch. After a while, after I gained more of Homeboy's trust, he had me runnin' errands for him and shit. I used to take the train all the way Uptown and get hit off wit' a supply from this little candy store up near Sugar Hill. I would put it in my math book, and shit. Homeboy took a likin' to me, and started teachin' me more and more of the business.

"I didn't know jack about makin' crack, but one day that nigga took me to the top of the Lab. It was the first time I'd ever been allowed upstairs, and he showed me mu'fuckas sitting at a table cutting that shit up. Then they'd push rocks into like this big bucket and pass the bucket to these other mu'fuckas at the next table and they would put the rocks into the crack vials. It's funny to think, but as much as I didn't know about the game, I was the one who got them to start thinkin' about recyclin'," a proud glint momentarily flashed through Benjamin's eyes as he recalled his innovation. "I was somewhere, I don't remember where, and I saw this bum taking his bottles into the grocery store for some nickels, and I thought, *damn,* instead of buying new vials we should just start payin' little kids a nickel a vial for each one they

189

brought to us--that shit worked like a charm.

"By the time I hit sixteen and they couldn't fuck wit' me no more, I was like 'fuck school!' I was on the case *twentyfourseven*. Bottlin' and sellin', bottlin' and sellin'. Then when that nigga got busted, he appointed me to run the lab, only sixteen years old, and I had moved all the way up the corporate ladder. I had mugs workin' for me, my little assault squad, shee-it, I was like mu'fuckin' Gotti out in this mu'fucka. We had shit on lock on this whole block. And now these Muslim mu'fuckas want me to give this shit up? Hard as I've mu'fuckin' worked for mine! Those niggaz mus' be crazy or dusted or sumptin'. But it really don't matter if they crazy or dusted, 'cauz we ain't givin' up jack shit. Them niggaz wanna trip, all right, we gon' trip."

The Trumpet Is Blown

Chapter Thirty-eight

He sees the hard concrete pavement drawing closer and closer, picking up steam. He hears the terrifying scream, rapidly plunging toward almost certain death; feels the horrifying crash of torn skin and broken bone. He's terrified. As a crowd gathers round the fallen body, the eerie wail of homicidal laughter haunts him.

Fiend wakes up drenched in sweat. He hadn't had this dream for years, having replaced it with crack fantasies, which were ultimately themselves displaced by horrifying crack-induced nightmares. Lately, the drug's numbing effect had waned as long-buried nightly horror stories of a plunging broken body had returned in full fury.

He felt strange. It was the first time he'd ever been inside the Mosque. Instead of worship, he was there for an N.A. meeting.

He had to make a change he had promised himself. There on the hard-tiled surface of the Mosque's basement, folk gathered every Thursday for support in their personal fight against addiction, attesting to the changes some had made and others hoped to make. Fiend sat in a seat in the back near the exit, already preparing to beat a hasty retreat. He'd even worn an old pair of shades, trying to conceal his identity. As the first person rose to speak, Fiend was nearly overwhelmed by skepticism, fear, and doubt and was tempted to bolt for the exit.

191

Somehow, though, he found the strength to stay.

"Boy, I'm glad to see so many people out tonight," the meeting's facilitator began. He was a young black man who looked to Fiend to be about the same age as him. He was fairly muscular and had a somewhat hard look about him--thick-necked, a faded, jagged scar around the mouth, rough hands and a gravelly voice; yet somehow he seemed at peace with himself, surprisingly happy. "Yes, I really am happy to see every one of you out here," he continued, "because I know what addiction does to you, man, believe me, I know. It does some strange shit to you. Let me tell you, even though I'm a male, yep, even though I'm a male ya'll, when I was doing that crack, I was suffering from p.m.s." The crowd laughed at the notion. "I'm tellin' ya'll, I had p.m.s.," he said, with a mock stern expression.

"Now I know a lot of ya'll don't believe me, but I'm tellin' you a lot of you men in here already have p.m.s., you just don't know it." He looked out on the crowd with a lot of disbelieving faces, not knowing where he was going, or what he was saying. And then he dropped it on them. "P.M.S., I'm tellin' ya'll: pain, misery and suffering."

He could see the look of recognition and acknowledgment on the faces of many of the newcomers, and he knew that he'd captured their attention as he'd hoped. And then he proceeded to tell them his sad spiraling tale of downward projection.

"You see, when I first started out, I wasn't even usin', I was just sellin', comin' home after

The Trumpet Is Blown

school, makin' some extra money, but then I saw how much money I was makin', and I said fuck school, I can do this full-time, and really get P-A-I-deed. Now, I was hustlin' full-time, I thought I was a little Nino Brown. Man, we used to make fun of the pookies, comin' up to us, beggin' for crack and shit. We'd make them do stupid shit, like jump up and down on one leg," he said, as he jumped up and down on one leg in demonstration, "bark like a dog, and then say in a Scooby Doo voice, 'Polly want some crack, sir'. And they'd do it, right there, in front of the whole block--they ain't have no shame. We were young and dumb--it was just a game to us. We'd smack them upside the head and tell them to get lost, no pay, no play. You see, the street seduced me, without me even knowin' it. Women comin' up to me offerin' me all kinds of favors, older women, women I never thought I had a chance with. And then I started believin' the hype, and that's when I crossed that line in the sand I had drawn. I started to believe I was invincible, and decided to try this crack shit. Shee-it, I figured I could handle it, I wasn't no pookie. At first it wasn't nuttin'--I just tried it and didn't try it again for a month. But, then about a month later, this beautiful woman who I'd fantasized about as a little kid came up to me for some crack. Now, she wasn't as beautiful as she once was, but she still was fine to me, and she promised me some sexual favors if I hooked her up and smoked some crack with her, so

I did, and that really set me off. The next thing I knew I started gettin' high on my own supply, as we say, and that's a no-no. No! No! You don't want to do that, I was fuckin' up business with the guys who put me down. They cut me off, but I had a need now. I had quit school, I ain't have no skills, so I started robbin', snatchin' pocketbooks off old women who couldn't fight back. By this time I didn't have nowhere to live either. When I was dealin' I could afford a piece of an apartment, but now, now, I was out on the street, sleepin' in the park, and it was startin' to get cold ya'll. My moms had kicked me out when I started dealin', and I was up shit's creek now, desperate. I went back to the block I used to run, I used to sell on, I was the man on, and asked for a freebie, for old time's sake, but them niggaz jus' laughed at me. And then one young nigga, who couldn't a been no more than thirteen, told me, me! To jump up and down on one leg, bark like a dog and say in a Scooby Doo voice, 'Polly want some crack, sir."

"Hmmph, hmmph, hmmph," you could here the crowd moan.

"I told him 'hell no, what did he think I was a pookie?' He said if I wasn't, I was doing the best impression he'd ever seen. I hated that little mutha . . ., but he was right. I walked away swearin' I'd never touch that shit again, but less than two hours later I couldn't believe it, I was standing there on one leg, jumping up and down, sayin' 'Polly want some crack, sir' in that Scooby Doo voice, and I always hated Scooby Doo," he said, with an ironic laugh. "After that I swore I'd never do it again, and I tried, I made three clean days after that, but I kept comin' back, I had to have the crack. Then one day, I spotted these three older women walkin' in the park, and one of them had a fat juicy pocketbook--it was too easy, I had to have it. I took off like Carl Lewis ya'll. I was movin', waitin' to snatch that baton, and then I ripped it out her hands, but she wouldn't let go. She wouldn't let go. I pulled so hard I drug her to the ground. That's when I heard a familiar voice say, "Son?" It was my mother--she had come to the park lookin' for me. That shit rocked me, I never felt so low. I kept runnin', pretending I hadn't heard her, pretending I didn't know it was her. Now, I had need on top of need, because I had to forget that shit, I had to forget what I had done, so I really had to get high. And then I got high, and I forgot--for a while, because that shit wears off; and when it wore off I felt lower than a pregnant ant. You know what we say, 'the higher the high, the lower the low'. I couldn't deal wit' that pain--I had snatched my own mother's pocketbook, and the shame was unbearable, but the only hope I saw was gettin' high all over again to forget again. I was trapped in a vicious, vicious cycle. I felt totally alone, frightened, and humiliated. I heard that niggaz who I'd conned into givin' me some crack on a loan type basis was lookin' for me 'cauz I was a week late in payin' them. I didn't know what to do, I had to get out of Brooklyn. So one night I snuck on the train to Manhattan because I didn't even have token money. And while I was on the train, I saw some brothas I used to go to high school wit' on a double date, havin' a good time, lookin' clean, crack free! And to think I used to think they were the suckers when I was dealin'. Now, I found myself duckin' into another car so they wouldn't see how low I had fallen. I know they saw me, but at least they gave me some respect and pretended they didn't. I managed to sell a pint of blood, and immediately ran to the crack man. I don't even know how I got there, but all I remember is the cop kickin' my feet tellin' me to wake up, they were clearing the park at midnight. When I opened my eyes, the view was all fuzzy, and I don't know, I guess I was still half-asleep fightin' those demons, and that cop looked like a monster to me, so I jus' sprung up off the bench and started to attack him. Don't you know that cop kicked my ass, busted my lip, gave me a black eye and bruised my ribs, but it was the best ass kickin' I ever got 'cause I found myself on Rikers. I'd never been to jail before, but being in there I was forced to go cold turkey. This brotha who worked there knew I was on crack and made me attend an N.A. outreach meeting. Of course, I didn't want to go--sheee-it, I wasn't no addict, as far as I was concerned--at least I wasn't ready to admit it yet, but he made me go. And when I went! And when I went, and I heard those stories, then I knew it was time to stop frontin', I was an addict. At that meeting I turned my life over to a power higher than myself. Eventually I got probation, by agreeing to go into a rehab program as soon as I got out. I went straight to a meeting, then I made one meeting a night for the next eighty-nine nights. Ninety meetings in ninety days. I've been clean for eighteen months now, I've got my G.E.D., I've got a regular pay check, and one day I'm going to college. I've got something to live for now, one day at a time."

"Hi, my name is Mark, I'm an addict, and I have thirty-six days in," he offered tentatively.

"Hi Mark, welcome," the crowd greeted him back, warmly and supportively.

"Hi, my name is Mu'min, and Ah'm an addict, and I have thirteen years in," he said humbly.

"Hi Mu'min, welcome," again the crowd responded with warm, supportive applause. Then the brotha who'd given the confessional spoke again.

"Whether you've been clean for eighteen months or eighteen days, it's still just one day at a time." Then he asked if there were any other newcomers who would like to declare themselves, while glancing at Fiend, who'd been enraptured by the striking similarity of the brotha's tale to his own.

In a rush of passionate emotion, Fiend, like Marcus before him, saw himself leap to his feet and declare, "Hi, my name is Curtis, and Ah'm an addict," but like Marcus before him he was still sitting. "Why am I still sitting?" he angrily asked himself. "Because you're not an addict," his pride falsely answered. "Shee-it, Ah'm not gettin' up in front of all these people and sayin' I'm no addict, I ain't no addict, I just got a little problem. Sheee-it, it ain't really a problem, I can stop." He was just like Marcus, at war

197

with himself, humility doing battle with pride, shame, and despair--and humility was once again losing. "Man, fuck this I ain't stayin' here, this is wack." He was up abruptly in a fit of anger, knocking over his chair, just as Marcus had done before him, and he started to storm out.

"Don't leave before the miracle happens," someone implored.

"It gets greater later," a seated sista shouted out to him, but their words were falling on deaf ears. Fiend didn't want to hear them, didn't want to acknowledge his problem, and unless he did, he was doomed.

"Don't leave, man, don't beat yourself up, give yourself a chance," a seated brotha implored.

"No, no, man," Fiend's unsteady cracking voice protested. "You, don't wanna help me, man, I'm a loser."

"You'll only be a loser if you walk outta here man. Please, I'm beggin' you man, give yourself a chance." There was a long unsteady silence as Fiend looked at the door anxiously, and then rushed out in tears.

Standing in the hallway, feeling confused and defeated, Fiend thought of Marcus. He sought escape shutting his eyes, but again saw Marcus diving toward the pavement. The sound of concrete breaking bone startled Fiend, causing him to shudder and his eyes to suddenly open violently. He shook his head soberly, recognizing there was nowhere to run, nowhere to hide.

The Trumpet Is Blown

"Hi, my name is Curtis," Fiend's voice boomed from the back of the room. "I'm an addict, and this is my first day here."

"Hi, Curtis, welcome," the crowd enthusiastically roared back, and then he was mobbed by a throng of well-wishers coming over to hug him, shake his hand, and well, wish him well. Fiend continued to cry, but his tears of sadness were now tears of joy. Maybe, he thought, there was a chance he could save himself after all.

David Lamb

Chapter Thirty-nine

Even after his seemingly triumphant N.A. meeting, the nightmare continued to haunt Curtis' dreams. He knew the cause. He'd been told by the people in N.A. that he had to get honest with himself and others, that he had to try and make amends for past wrongs, that he had to stop beating himself up, had to let go of his guilt; but it was too big a burden.

The only way he could really unburden himself, he knew, was to finally reveal the painful truth that had haunted him for so long; but he was afraid, even though he knew that holding it in was slowly killing him.

The next day he spent the whole day just walking--nowhere in particular, just walking and thinking, thinking and walking. He saw people looking at him like he was crazy because he was mumbling to himself; but his thoughts were too intense to hold in, he had to get them out and didn't care what people thought. Sometime around three a.m., he managed to find his way back around the projects, but he realized that he couldn't go back to that apartment. He collapsed in exhaustion at the back of the same alley where Sharrief had previously chased him down. Fighting sleep for fear of the nightmare's return, Curtis slowly succumbed to its seductive powers. Before long the horrifying, shrill scream of Marcus plunging toward the rapidly rising concrete was once again terrorizing his conscience. Laying in a pool of his own sweat, Curtis began to hear voices all around him. He couldn't tell where they were coming from, but they were all around him! He was terrified as the voices grew louder, stronger, angrier. He awoke cuddling himself in his arms, shaking, but the voices were still all around him, ever angrier. He looked around in confusion and fear, waiting for the bodies attached to the voices to attack him. None came. Slowly his mind was able to detect that the voices were rushing toward him from the other end of the alley. He sat up carefully, nervously listening in where he had no business listening.

"I told you about going behind my back questioning my mu'fuckin' orders, mu'fucka, right, right?!" Benjamin's voice was rising with anger and taking on an increasingly menacing tone.

"I . . . I . . . I"

"I nothin' mu'fucka, ain't that right?!"

"I wasn't questioning . . ." J-Son pleaded.

"Oh so you sayin' that Mic-Boogie is lyin'?!"

"Oh, Ah'm lyin', mu'fucka?!" Mic-Boogie yelled from a place that sounded to Curtis somewhere right behind Benjamin.

"No, no . . ."

"No, no what mu'fucka? Speak now or forever hold your peace." Benjamin ordered.

"I . . . I," J-Son swallowed hard, he was afraid to speak, "I . . . I was jus'. . . I was jus'. . ."

"You was jus' what mu'fucka?"

"I was jus' sayin', you know, why, why, why," in his nervousness he kept repeating his words, "I was

jus' sayin' why, why fuck wit' these niggaz? We
could just move our shit a coupla blocks over where
ain't nobody tryin'a be no hero."

"See mu'fucka," Benjamin chuckled in
disbelief, while glancing back at Glock, Mic-Boogie,
and Beast. "See what happens when mu'fucka's start
tryin'a be creative instead of following orders?" J-Son
was standing opposite the rest of the crew, shivering,
and scared witless. "See, this is how mu'fuckas get
taken down, people not following the plan. Now, I
done explained to niggaz, we takin' these mu'fuckaz
out tomorrow, period, 'cause we can't let them have
this block 'cause then mu'fuckaz everywhere will start
gettin' brave and shit, so we got to stop these
mu'fuckaz right here and now! I thought you wanted
to be a playa, but I see now, you jus' a little sucka.
And I can't have suckaz on my team. I can't have
suckaz on my team."

Benjamin's verbal assault was suddenly
interrupted by the clashing sound of falling garbage
tops. "Who the fuck is back there?" Glock barked
quickly, drawing his nine from his crotch.

"Don't shoot . . . Don't shoot," Curtis pleaded
as he rose, shaking, with his hands up and fearful eyes
cast down.

"I . . . I . . . I heard what ya'll was talkin'
about," he said through his fear and mental fog.

"Yo' man, I tol' you to leave that crack shit
alone, you buggin'. What's up wit' that, you confusin'
your dreams wit' reality nigga? You best to get a
check up from the neck up," Benjamin said

dismissively.

"I know what I heard," Curtis said, his voice trembling.

"Oh! Oh! So you callin' me a liar, nigga? You callin' me a liar?"

"Yo', yo' Fiend, you want some crack man? Come here, let me hook you up," Glock teased, holding a plastic package of about twenty small yellow-capped vials in his right hand shaking them so hard they hissed like rattlesnakes. "Come here let me hook you up," Glock said enticingly. The lure of the crystalline talismans pulled at Curtis' basest desires. Memories of euphoric crack highs danced in his head. "Just one more hit," he thought, "just one more hit." He would have taken one more hit, but he remembered the brother snatching his own mother's pocketbook, he remembered the catastrophic post crack-binge lows, and he resisted. He resisted.

"Don't front nigga, you know you want some of this," Glock insisted, dangling the package of vials no more than two inches from Curtis' eyes which looked longingly at his former love.

"Look," Curtis continued, averting his eyes from the crack and gazing at Benjamin, "look, I know."

"You know nothing!" Benjamin yelled furiously. "You know nothing, nigga! You know. Talkin' 'bout you know, you know nothin'. Only thing you know is how to light up, mu'fucka." Laughter filtered through the air. "Now, see you gettin' in my business and you know I don't like people gettin' in my business, so I suggest you get your pookie ass out of here before you get hurt."

"Yeah," Glock added, kicking Curtis where the sun don't shine, causing his pants to rise up a little as if he were pulling them up to go into the water at the beach. "Get movin' nigga," Glock ordered as he shoved Curtis out the alley.

"But . . ."

"Yo' nigga, you heard what he said," Mic-Boogie yelled, smacking Curtis with the back of his hand, knocking him hard, driving him to the pavement reopening the cut on his top lip. "Get, the fuck up!" Mic-Boogie yelled, sweeping Curtis' feet out from under him as he tried to stand, causing him to fall back to the ground on his back in a loud, thudding crash.

"Shee-it," Benjamin said, "I told you to get out of here before you get hurt, capisce?"

Curtis looked up and saw a smiling Glock standing over him, waving the plastic bag. His eyes followed it round and round in a hypnotic trance. He was at wit's end, he knew that Benjamin was capable of anything. He was confused. Why should he put himself on the line? Solace was inches from his hands. He reached up and took the plastic bag. In the background thunderous, sarcastic applause broke out, as Curtis crawled out of the alley feeling both despair and relief.

He walked around in a state of confusion for hours until he found himself back in the alley. His legs hurt, his ankles hurt, his head ached. He sat for a moment in the corner before blacking out. As he started to lose consciousness, he remembered Marcus. Remembered that like Jibril, Shaun, and Benjamin, he and Marcus, along with their own gang of little rascals, used to play football in the project grass. Remembered that he'd even tried to imitate Marcus' style. Marcus had a certain charisma. He was tall and handsome, and always had the first pick with the girls. His first double date was with Marcus, they'd taken some girls to see *New Jack City*. It wasn't long after that that Curtis started rising in the game. Up to that time he and Marcus had on occasion shared a little weed on darkened back staircases, but when crack came in, that was another animal all together. Soon enough, the money started rolling in. He wanted Marcus to be part of the team, not a customer. "Why did he have to start using?" he asked himself. He hadn't meant to hurt Marcus, he just wanted to scare him, to make sure he paid up. Benjamin had other ideas however. He wanted to make an example out of Marcus so people would know that he didn't take any shorts.

Once again caught in the middle, he didn't know what to do. Drifting further into lost consciousness he saw himself laying in a pile of dung, his right hand ladened with skulls and bones. All around horrifying screams abounded. Slowly a piercing sound began penetrating his consciousness.

As the eerie wail of the trumpet rose slowly, it was accompanied by an increasingly brilliant blinding light, and as the horn reached a soaring crescendo a sudden shocking light burst, momentarily blinded him. As his vision slowly returned, Curtis saw himself kneeling with his head bowed and his hands cupped behind his back, his right hand grasping his left wrist. He couldn't see where he was. There was a fine white fog-like mist all around, enveloping him. He felt his memories being pulled from his deepest subconscious against his will; he'd thought that they were secrets he'd carry to his grave. Kneeling there, he felt his own memories being used to condemn him. On the floor in front of him was a large magenta book with gold lettering, the cover said simply: READ.

Although he did not actually hear anyone speaking, he kept hearing the word 'read' repeated, faster and louder until finally he had to, or he would go insane. When he opened the book the cover page said simply: The Balance. The second page of the book contained one simple phrase: 'He who has done an atom's weight of good shall see it. And he who has done an atom's weight of evil shall see it.' Then he heard his own voice, coming from deep within himself, say: 'Read thy book. Your own conscience is enough as a witness against you this day.' Curtis cried out in vain protest, hearing similar desperate pleas all around him. He pleaded that he not be made to see, but fighting against his own conscience was painfully futile. As he turned the pages he saw himself snatching his first pocketbook, dragging some old silver-haired white woman down the block. He saw himself smoking crack, finally he saw Marcus tumbling off the roof.

The Trumpet Is Blown

Waking up drenched in his own sweat, Curtis looked down and saw his right hand cradling the plastic bag full of crack vials. He was tempted, just for a moment, but he dropped the bag, stood up and watched his foot come crashing down on the bag, crushing the vials until finally he began dancing a happy dance all over that bag. Snatching it up, he heaved it into the garbage. He didn't want to betray his brother, but he knew what he had to do.

Jibril had just finished helping his mom carry the groceries inside when Curtis knocked on his door. As he looked through the peephole, Jibril blurted out, "What the hell?"

"What is it?" his mother exclaimed.

"Oh it's nothing, just my man," he said trying to sound calm, as he stepped into the hallway, closing the door behind.

"Jibril, I have to tell you something, something I've been carrying around for a long time. Be careful with Benjamin, Jibril." Curtis' voice was solemn and Jibril was shocked by how clear his eyes looked and how lucid he sounded.

"What?" Jibril asked impatiently, almost threateningly.

"Be careful . . ." reiterated Curtis, he was fighting elaborating.

"What are you talkin' about?"

"I know ya'll tryin' to shut him down and all and that's positive, but be careful, that nigga's not right upstairs." Jibril wondered why Fiend was telling

207

David Lamb

him this now.

"Huh?" he asked in bewilderment.

"That nigga's crazy, he'll do anything to stay on top." The whites of Curtis' eyes, unseen for years, widened in fear.

"Man, I ain't worried about him," Jibril responded.

"No, you don't understand--that nigga's crazy," taking a deep breath, his heart racing anxiously, Curtis finally relieved himself of the terrible burden he'd been carrying. "Jibril, Marcus didn't fall off that roof, he was pushed. He was pushed."

The Trumpet Is Blown

Chapter Forty

Since its inception weeks before, on any given night, anywhere from eighteen to twenty-six brothas from Al-Qiyamah, led by Imam Aziz and joined by Charlie Stokes, had been patrolling a three block radius around the Mosque. Armed with faith and steely resolve, they walked among the ruins, standing out by their numbers, their multicolored kufis glowing under the glare of street lamps.

If he didn't do something now this would be not only the fourth week, but the fourth Thursday in a row that Benjamin's business took a dip on what was normally his most profitable night. He was furious. J-Son, acting against his natural instincts, had pissed him off by suggesting that perhaps they move their operation somewhere else, where there was less resistance. The subsequent beat-down he received at the hands of Beast, acting on Benjamin's orders, served to remind J-Son to follow his inclinations. Benjamin had told his boys to hold back when the patrol first began, figuring that they'd run out of steam after a few days. Now he was thinking that he'd made a mistake; the Muslims were growing too bold, rolling on his employees--telling them that they couldn't do business around there anymore. Shit, this was *his* neighborhood!

"See! See, muthafucka!" He shouted as if to psyche himself up. "Now, they done got a nigga pissed off. All right, all right, those stupid ass niggaz wanna try and play Jackie Chan. Okay, we gonna see what happens when one of them muthafuckas tries to block a Black Talon. What Richard Pryor say? Them muthafuckas can't wait to get to Allah, okay, they don't have to wait, we'll send them along now. Shee-it, they sleeping on the street. Man, fuck that, Ah'm tryin'a blow up like the World Trade, and them niggaz gettin' in my way, we gonna have to deal wit' them once and for all."

Sitting there on his bed staring out the window, Benjamin cuddled his girl. He liked them like her, short and powerfully built, with a large butt, yet graceful, sleek, and easy to control. When he held her, he felt powerful. She always had his back. And on top of everything she loved to get down and dirty. He loved to open her up, explore her with his fingers, stabbing and poking her barrel, digging deep, cleaning her out with a moist Q-tip, squinting his eyes to look inside, oiling her springs and racking her slide. Treat your lady right, and she'll treat you right. That's what the brotha who sold her to him had said, you've got to take care of her or when the time comes for her to back you up, she won't. He always took good care of his lady, 'cause he never knew when he'd need her. He aimed her, pulling back on her tender spot, pretending to fire her at an invisible target. "Take that motherfucker," he said, before reassuringly blowing into the barrel and kissing his bride.

Landa hadn't seen Jibril since he'd stopped by her house, but it didn't matter, she wasn't thinking about him at the moment anyway. She was looking for Benjamin. He'd promised to take her up to City Island for some shrimp scampi and they were supposed to have met at six o'clock. He still hadn't called despite the fact that she'd beeped him several times and punched in her special code: 669. She was growing impatient.

Not as impatient as Shaun who was on his way home from his sixth mail-room job interview in two days. He'd spent much of the last month avoiding Benjamin, who had told Shaun that he couldn't quit the game until he'd paid back the $1,100 he owed Benjamin in phony accumulated debt. Shaun had been staying at his cousin's house up in the Bronx (where the people are fresh) trying to plan his next move. He hadn't seen his son in over a month and since it was Thursday he figured that Benjamin would be busy and that he'd be able to slip in and out without being seen.

"Bye daddy," Lil' Shaun's squeaky voice echoed in the hall as Shaun kissed his baby's mother on the cheek. Before he left, Shaun couldn't help picking his son up again and tossing him in the air in a game they'd long shared. Finally able to tear himself away, he happily jogged down the steel staircase. The cadence of his own footsteps reminded Shaun of his locale and he decided to tread more softly.

Treading softly was the furthest thing from Landa's mind as she stormed out of her door determined to tell Benjamin off for standing her up.

Years before, after storming the monkey bars

at the neighborhood playground, Shaun, Benjamin, Chris, and Landa played in the cold water that spewed from the blow hole in the metal blue whale decorating the kiddie park, taking turns teaming up and chasing each other, trying to force one another to sit on the hole. As dinner time approached, they'd race each other back to their buildings laughing hysterically as their wet sneakers pounded the pavement.

Now, it was hardly a laughing matter when Shaun and Landa arrived out of their respective buildings at the same time. Spotting Landa first, Shaun's eyes bulged wildly with fear, as he swiftly turned in the other direction ducking back in the building lobby, not wanting to risk Landa telling Benjamin that she saw him. Shaun waited until the coast looked clear, then continued quickly to the nearest subway station, while trying to appear the cool and calm brotha he was not at the moment.

He couldn't put his finger on it, but Shaun sensed something different in the air, somehow he just knew that it wasn't going to be a normal night.

Unlike Shaun, Benjamin Franklin could put his finger on it, right on the trigger. He knew it wasn't going to be a normal night. "This patrol bullshit had gone too far," he said. He needed to get his business back on track.

"All right Glock, you and that nigga Mic-Boogie gonna come at 'em from that side of the street. Ah'm a be up on that roof right there keepin' watch, and bustin' a cap in anybody who gets by you or even comes close."

212

The Trumpet Is Blown

Since he'd spent the last month laying low in the Bronx, Shaun didn't know anything about the patrol. He was shocked when he saw Landa again, this time standing thirty feet in front of him impatiently waiting for the patrol to move on so that she could be on her merry way. He wondered what was going on. As Landa brushed past the patrol, Shaun quickly followed behind hoping to get a closer glimpse of the patrol, when Curtis suddenly came running up to him in a panic.

"Yo' Fiend step off, nigga, I ain't got no crack for your dirty ass!" Shaun said harshly.

"Listen," Curtis said frantically, "it's not about that, it's about Jibril."

"What you talkin' about?" Shaun asked in confusion, the last person he expected Fiend to be talking about was Jibril.

"Listen, you've got to stop him," trying to catch his breath, Curtis paused between words.

"Stop him? From doing what?"

"He knows," Curtis managed between exhausted breaths.

"Knows what?"

"He . . . he knows. He knows Marcus didn't jump off that roof."

"Aw shit!" Shaun exclaimed throwing both arms up in frustration. "Aw shit, why'd you do that, man? Where's he at?!"

"I don't know, he ran out. I guess he's looking for Benjamin."

Shaun shielded his eyes from the glare of the

street lamps, squinting as he looked down the block. Just then he was struck by Benjamin's shadowy figure crouching on a nearby roof. Shaun immediately knew the deal--it was an ambush. He searched the block for Glock, fixing his gaze on a silver sparkle coming from the burnt out vestibule of an abandoned building on the left side of the street. Looking back at the patrol, he saw Jibril trying to catch up to the end of the patrol. Without thinking, he raced down the block yelling to Jibril to duck. Hearing his familiar voice and frantic cries, Landa ran back to inspect the happenings. Knowing that their cover had been blown, Glock and Mic-Boogie emerged from the vestibule firing. Jibril hit the ground. Charlie Stokes hit the ground. Benjamin hit the safety clip on his gun, undoing it, and came up firing; everyone ran for cover. Shaun ran toward Jibril trying to lead him to safety. A bullet meant for the young trumpeter's head found a home in Shaun's flesh. Jibril glanced up and saw a smiling Benjamin, his gun trained on him, fire.

Jibril thought he was dead.

When he opened his eyes, he saw Benjamin wrestling with his gun, jammed by the recycled bullets he'd been using. Seizing the moment, he sprinted toward the building where Benjamin was firing from and raced up the steps. Unable to fix his gun, Benjamin tucked it in his pants and headed for the stairs, where he was greeted by Jibril's straight right hand.

As he looked up, groggily, from his new found position on the floor, Benjamin deftly avoided Jibril's

The Trumpet Is Blown

Timberland angrily speeding toward him, bounded to his feet and sprang at Jibril, driving him into the brick wall, raising a rapidly rising knot on the back of Jibril's head. Knocking him to the floor, Benjamin lunged toward Jibril, pinning his arms and shoulders under his knees, as he'd once seen Priest do. "What now muthafucka?" he demanded wildly. "Huh Superman?" he taunted. "What now punk? I don't hear you sayin' shit now! Huh, muthufucka!" Shit, he was right, Jibril had to admit. He wasn't saying anything, he was too busy trying to get Benjamin off of him. "Oh tryin' to get me off you, huh, mu'fucka? Momma's boy!" Jibril saw Benjamin's tightly balled fist zoom at him with rocket-like speed. With all his strength Jibril managed to lift Benjamin's left leg and move his head just in time to avoid the punch. As his fist met concrete, Benjamin howled in pain, and Jibril took advantage of the moment to toss Benjamin completely off of him. Both sprang back to their feet, squared off, Benjamin reached for his gun. Jibril reached to stop him. They wrestled violently--then suddenly Benjamin's gun exploded in fury.

Landa, standing at the stairwell entrance to the roof lunged at Jibril and screamed a haunting, echoing, "N o o o o o o o !" Benjamin dropped to his knees clutching his bleeding abdomen. Jibril was in shock as Landa screamed, "You killed him! You killed him!"

215

David Lamb

You always say,
"Don't tell me,
I have eyes,
I can see,"
and I think to myself
tis' true you have eyes,
but I never saw you see

The Trumpet Is Blown

Chapter Forty-one

"Yo' it's bugged how those niggaz' guns got jammed," Beast said slyly. "I heard Mic-Boogie's gun blew up in his hands, and that Glock didn't get off but one shot before his gun stopped."

"They were constipated," J-Son joked. "Wonder how that happened?" he said knowingly.

"Yeah wonder?"

They both laughed. "But for real though, I wasn't sure what was up. When Benjamin called for that meetin', I thought that was our ass--that they'd found out about the barbershop."

"Nah, I told you I wasn't sweatin' it, he was too suped to think that anybody would test him. He always had to do things the difficult way. That nigga was too much into conflict. I told him let's roll over here where niggaz ain't tryin'a be heroes. I warned them niggaz. Fuck it, that shit is done. Yo', today we gonna celebrate we back in business, two for one on jumbos, we got money to make."

217

David Lamb

Chapter Forty-two

"Okay Jibril it all comes down to this. You're a better player than all these other guys, just stay calm, stay focused, concentrate." Nsinga whispered to Jibril offering him final backstage encouragement. I . . . I . . . I . . . I . . . I have something . . . I made something for you. Here." Nervously reaching into her pocket, her hand slightly quivering from her anxiety, she slowly pulled out a small velvet case, quietly passing the box from her hands to his palm.

"What is it?" he asked.

"Open it." Opening it slowly, Jibril first saw the coiled silver links and then the heart. He was stunned but managed to say, "It's beautiful."

"Look at it . . . See?"

"Wow! It's not a piercing arrow, it's a piercing trumpet."

"I made it just for you. Look at the back."

"What's it say?"

"It's Chinese, Jimmy Chin wrote out the symbols for me."

"Wow . . ."

"It means take good care of my heart."

"Take good care of my heart?"

"Yes, take good care of my heart. You're the first to take it, the only one who could break it. Take good care of my heart. Here, let me put it on."

Returning her tenderness with a warm gaze, Jibril looked deeply into her eyes as she fastened the pendant, gently lifted her hands placing them softly against his heart. Looking still more deeply into her eyes, Jibril said softly, "Take good care of mine."

Standing on the stage getting ready to play, Jibril tried to calm himself. As he looked into the crowd he saw those he admired and hoped to play with, those who'd loved and encouraged him, and those he'd loved and encouraged. He saw his mother smiling, her face beaming with pride. As he continued to look out, he saw Bilal flash a peace sign, and then had to laugh when he saw Jimmy from the No-Pork Chinese restaurant, sitting between Bilal and Carlos. His heart was warmed when he saw Shaun limp in using his new cane, flashing Jibril the "V for victory" sign.

All of Hassan's lessons appeared before Jibril's mind's eye flying fast and furious. He remembered going to Hassan's for those first lessons, and the first thing Hassan made him do was go running. He had been pretty upset, after all, he'd come to learn to play the trumpet. If he wanted to run he could've gone to the basketball court.

Nevertheless, Hassan persisted. "The trumpet is a wind instrument," he explained. "You've got to have stamina and be in shape in order to play it." So Jibril relented, sure that he'd get to play after going running. Instead of playing, though, he spent the next three days spitting unpopped popcorn kernels into a paper bag. He had been really upset about this. On top of not playing, it just seemed entirely too bizarre, but again Hassan insisted that it was necessary in order for Jibril to develop the proper embouchure, the

David Lamb

characteristic trumpet lip positioning, in order to play correctly. Finally, he finished with the popcorn and was ready to play, or so he thought, but before he'd get to work with the whole trumpet, Hassan teased him with just the mouthpiece to practice with. "What's this supposed to be?!" he'd demanded in angry frustration. Again Hassan, in his calm dignified manner, his dark brown eyes peering through his glasses, his grey temples suggesting sagacity, gently explained to Jibril that before he could work with the trumpet as a whole instrument, he first had to master the mouthpiece. Hassan insisted that Jibril had to develop his embouchure, since that was the key to great trumpet playing. He taught him how to tuck his lips closely around his teeth, leaving a small hole for the air column he'd have to bring up from his diaphragm--right up to the mouthpiece in order to create the buzz necessary to play. Despite Hassan's explanation, Jibril stubbornly insisted that he be allowed to put the mouthpiece in the trumpet, so Hassan relented. After several painfully futile attempts, a winded and embarrassed Jibril took the mouthpiece out of the trumpet, put the trumpet down, walked over to the basement window, looked out and began the necessary practice to create that buzz.

When he could finally buzz like a bee, he got to play. But Jibril wanted to look cool, and Hassan had to constantly fight with him to stand and sit properly when playing. Jibril wanted to bend over and twist, exaggeratedly contorting both his body and his face, a style more reminiscent of Jodeci than Dizzy.

220

The Trumpet Is Blown

Hassan wasn't having it, not from someone just learning to play. "You're not playing to be seen," he'd say, "you're playing to be heard, now fly right," he'd say, leaving off the euphemistic "straighten up and". Whenever he'd say "fly right," Jibril would know to fix his posture. Now Jibril, on the precipice of what lies before, took a deep breath, said a silent prayer, and closed his eyes. "Fly right," he said.